HOOK'S REVENGE

ALSO BY HEIDI SCHULZ
The Pirate Code

HOOK's REVENGE

by **HEIDI SCHULZ**

with illustrations by **JOHN HENDRIX**

DISNEP • HYPERION

LOS ANGELES   NEW YORK

SCH

Text copyright © 2014 by Heidi Schulz
Illustrations copyright © 2014 by John Hendrix

All rights reserved. Published by Disney•Hyperion, an imprint of Disney Book Group. No part of this book may be reproduced or transmitted in any form or by any means, electronic or mechanical, including photocopying, recording, or by any information storage and retrieval system, without written permission from the publisher. For information address Disney•Hyperion, 125 West End Avenue, New York, New York 10023-6387.

Printed in the United States of America
First Hardcover Edition, September 2014
First Paperback Edition, September 2015
10 9 8 7 6 5 4 3 2 1
J689-1817-1-15166

Library of Congress Control Number for Hardcover: 2013045281
ISBN 978-1-4847-1188-0
Visit www.DisneyBooks.com

SUSTAINABLE FORESTRY INITIATIVE

Certified Chain of Custody
Promoting Sustainable Forestry

www.sfiprogram.org
SFI-01054

The SFI label applies to the text stock

For Walt, who stole my heart the second time we met
and keeps it still

And for Hannah, who knew this was hers
but demanded it anyway

Pirates, both

CONTENTS

Children Have Sticky Fingers and Ask Impertinent Questions

There have always been pirates. Why, even as far back as Eve, on the day she was considering whether or not to eat that apple, a pirate was most certainly planning to sail in and take it from her.

I expect that you'd like to know about the most famous of all pirates, Captain James Hook. As I am the world's foremost expert on him, naturally you turned to me. Children come to me all the time, begging to hear what I know. I graciously seat them in a circle around me, lean in, and whisper, "Not a chance."

I don't like children all that much.

However, last Thursday I became an old man. It occurs to me that someday I will die. Like many my age, I hope that I may go peacefully, in the midst of a hostage situation or a failed arson attempt. But I digress. . . .

We were talking about Captain Hook.

Most everyone knows the main points of his story: Peter Pan, the iron hook, the crocodile, and so on and so forth. What came after, however—with Jocelyn, Hook's last request, and such—now, that's far more interesting.

What's that? You've never heard of young Jocelyn Hook?

I'm not surprised. I'd venture to guess that a list of things you know nothing about could fill volumes. However, today appears to be your lucky day—you are about to be enlightened. The fact that I am the one who must provide the enlightenment can only mean that today is my unlucky day, but sometimes these things cannot be helped.

There is no use putting it off any longer; it is time to tell what I know, lest the girl's story die with me. Settle in, I suppose. Do be sure not to touch anything, and for heaven's sake, please don't breathe so loudly. If you're quite comfortable, I'll pour myself a little drink and begin. If you are not comfortable, I'll begin anyway. Your comfort is of little concern to me.

CHAPTER ONE

*In Which Our Heroine Displays a
Clear Need for Professional Help*

The week before Jocelyn's grandfather decided to send her away to finishing school was an eventful one, even by her standards.

On Monday, the girl's newest tutor found his pupil unable to do her history lesson. Someone had torn most of the pages from her lesson book in order to make paper boats. This same unidentified person had then floated the paper vessels on the garden pond, after lighting them on fire, of course. Jocelyn sat at her desk, the very picture of wide-eyed innocence—with a spot of soot on her nose and the faint smell of smoke still clinging to her rumpled dress.

If you ask me, her tutor was wrong to turn in his resignation. True history is filled with burning fleets.

On Tuesday, Jocelyn startled the head cook, who

rather foolishly did not expect a twelve-year-old girl to come flying down the front banister brandishing a wooden sword and singing a bawdy sea chantey at the top of her lungs. A tea tray of French pastries dropped on the manor's finest Persian rug was clearly no one's fault but the cook's own.

Wednesday, Thursday, and Friday were much the same: Jocelyn tore her new silk stockings trying to climb the high iron fence surrounding Hopewell Manor in order to see out and "scout for enemy ships approaching." Her finest blue sash went missing, only to be discovered beneath the hedgerow, one end tied into a complicated sailor's knot, the other a noose. She even scandalized the third-floor serving maids by refusing her evening bath with a shouted "Look out, ye dog-livered landlubbers! I'm the most feared girl pirate to ever live! I'll see you keelhauled before you get me to walk the plank!"

All these things were bad, to be sure, but not entirely out of character for the girl. It was what she did on Saturday that made Sir Charles Hopewell IV, Jocelyn's grandfather and guardian, feel he had to take drastic action.

On that fateful day, Sir Charles invited Lord and Lady Trottington and their one-day-perhaps-quite-eligible son, Ambrose, to a dinner party in order to show off his lovely young granddaughter. To his great dismay, the evening did not go as well as he had hoped.

Jocelyn sauntered into the dining room twenty minutes after the soup course had been served, with twigs in her unruly dark curls, muddy knees, grass stains on the seat of her dress, and a tattered adventure novel tucked under her arm. Her grandfather glowered at her and muttered something under his breath about interviewing for yet another governess as soon as possible.

Jocelyn laughed at his scowl, plopped her book down on the sideboard, and seated herself directly across from Ambrose. She couldn't help but see that the young gentleman was unabashedly picking his nose. She stared in fascinated interest. Ambrose took no notice but continued with his mining.

"I am sorry for coming in late," Jocelyn said to the boy, "but I was lost in the best part of my book. A giant Cyclops threatened to eat Odysseus and his crew. In order to escape and return to their ship, they had to get the monster drunk, wait until he was firmly asleep, find a sharp stick, and"—Jocelyn leaned in and spoke in a reverential whisper—"gouge his terrible Cyclops eye out. Isn't that marvelous?"

Ambrose yawned. He did not bother to remove his finger from his nostril, choosing instead to speak around it. "That's rather disgusting talk for the dining table." His sinus spelunking paused for the briefest of moments while he looked Jocelyn over. "You are pretty enough, I suppose, but I can see that you may need to learn some manners if we are to court when we are older."

Jocelyn immediately decided dinner should not last much longer. If Ambrose wanted a display of manners, she would give him one. For the next quarter of an hour the girl laughed too loudly, slurped her soup, dribbled gravy in her lap, and used her sleeve instead of a napkin.

Sir Charles and Lord Trottington took no notice; they were deep in discussion about the proper application of wig powder. Lady Trottington examined the quality of the silverware with an expression of silent disapproval. Ambrose removed his finger from his nose and inserted it in his ear. He pulled out a sticky glob of wax, sniffed it, and wiped it on the tablecloth.

Clearly, it was time for Jocelyn to play her trump card.

"You know," she said in a loud voice, "I think my father would like to meet you. He's been away, but I expect he'll come for me anytime now. Perhaps you have heard of him? Captain James Hook?"

Lady Trottington fainted dead away into her plate of jellied eels. Lord Trottington let out a terrified scream. (Who would have guessed him to be a soprano?) As for Ambrose, the thorough scrubbing a housemaid gave his chair later that evening stood as testament to his reaction to Jocelyn's pronouncement.

The next day, Sir Charles demanded that his grand-daughter take an unusual outing with him: a stroll down execution dock. After a public hanging, the bodies of pirates and other criminals were placed in iron cages, called gibbets, and put on display. Sir Charles planned to employ a time-honored tactic used by parents the world over: frightening the child into obedience.

As the pair walked along the dock, a horrifying scene played out above them. The gibbets creaked and moaned as they swayed, calling to mind the sounds of ghosts in all the old stories.

Their occupants varied in looks, depending on fresh-ness. Those that had been long exposed to the elements were reduced to little more than rags and bones. Skulls grinned down at the gentleman and his granddaughter, empty eye sockets staring. Worse still were the remains of the more recently deceased. Some had swelled so much that they pressed into the bars, rather like an overly ample woman trying to squeeze into a too-small corset.

A few moments of the terrible view ought to have been sufficient. Sir Charles pressed a handkerchief to his nose and ushered the willful child back to the safety of their carriage. They traveled most of their way home in silence. As the pair reached the manor gates, Sir Charles, wanting to be sure of his success, questioned his grand-daughter: "And what did you learn today, Jocelyn?"

The girl looked up at him with red-rimmed eyes. "Two things, Grandfather. First, if I am to be a pirate and sail with my father, I must be a very good one and not get caught. Second, I will never, ever wear a corset."

That very evening, Sir Charles penned a letter to Miss Eliza Crumb-Biddlecomb herself. Even with his best efforts, he had been unable to make any headway in turning Jocelyn into a lady. It was time for professional help.

CHAPTER TWO

First Impressions Can Be Wrong,
But Usually Aren't

Life is full of disappointments. Chocolates melt or are eaten by rodents. Ponies die. Kittens grow into cats—and cats are such hateful creatures. However, when Jocelyn arrived at the place that her grandfather intended to be her home, school, and prison for years to come, she was not disappointed: it was just as terrible as the girl had expected.

She hated every bit of the place, from its ivy-covered stone walls to the gilded lettering on its front-door sign:

MISS ELIZA CRUMB-BIDDLECOMB'S
FINISHING SCHOOL FOR YOUNG LADIES.

Well-groomed walks and lawns were populated by well-groomed young ladies strolling arm in arm or lounging on stone benches. The happy burbling of a nearby brook harmonized with the thrum of humming-bird wings as they flitted among fragrant garden flowers. Fireflies floated up, their lights twinkling in the early-evening shadows.

Jocelyn fought the urge to be sick.

She was in the midst of formulating a complicated escape plan involving a spade fork and a pair of croquet mallets when a stern-looking lady emerged from the school and began issuing orders. This could only be Miss Eliza Crumb-Biddlecomb. Jocelyn turned to face the headmistress, forcing herself to look the woman in the eye.

Miss Eliza did not waste time on pleasantries. "I hope you took refreshment on the road. You are nearly one quarter hour past the end of dinner, and we do not reopen the kitchens until morning. No exceptions. Breakfast will be at eight o'clock, sharp. Dress smartly and be punctual. Latecomers will not be served. No exceptions."

Jocelyn had not yet had dinner. When her stomach received word that there would be none, and that the prospect of breakfast was threatened as well, it let out an angry growl.

Miss Eliza gave the girl a pointed look and went on.

"I have sent your trunks up to your room. A chamber-maid will unpack them and air your clothing. You will be sharing a suite with Miss Priscilla Edgeworth and Miss Nanette Arbuckle. We do not offer private accommodations here. No exceptions."

Jocelyn fidgeted, only half listening.

"All the young ladies are currently enjoying some free time. I will have you shown to your suite momentarily, where you will have a few minutes to prepare to greet your roommates. I suggest you use your time wisely and employ some soap and water. Your face and hands are rather dusty from your travels. You must not fail to put your best foot forward."

Jocelyn stole a glance at her hands. They weren't exactly spotless, but since she had been cooped up in the carriage most of the day, they were a good sight cleaner than usual.

Miss Eliza continued with her speech. "Your grandfather has written me regarding some of your peculiarities, but I have assured him that you are not a hopeless case. It is not unusual for a girl growing up without the benefit of a mother to have some rough patches. Fortunately, I am quite experienced in filing down rough patches. I have been headmistress of this school for nearly three decades. In that time many a young lady has appeared at my door, unrefined in either manners, appearance, or both. Not once have I failed to turn the girl into a lady worthy of her class and distinction. No exceptions."

Miss Eliza stood for a moment longer, silently appraising the girl.

"You may go now. I expect you are feeling tired from your journey."

Jocelyn gave Miss Eliza her most irksome smile and replied, "Actually, I'm feeling rather *exceptional*," then turned heel and followed the chambermaid to her room, taking care to scuff her shoes on the polished wood flooring the whole way.

Her room was a monstrosity of pink.

The walls were papered in a soft mauve with a sickening pattern of sweet little roses. Three fluffy chairs, upholstered in pale carnation, sat before a rose-colored Italian marble fireplace. Jocelyn's trunks were neatly stacked at the foot of a frilly bed: delicate pink coverlets under soft pink canopies surrounded by deep pink curtains.

It will be like sleeping in a giant mouth, she thought with disgust.

Two identical atrocities were lined up next to it. Jocelyn pulled back the bed curtains to inspect them. They did not appear to be occupied, but she jumped on each mattress a time or two, to be certain.

Smart thinking, that. You can never be too careful.

The room's remaining furniture also came in triplicate, and in pink. Three wardrobes, painted puce, next to three matching dressing tables beneath three coral-colored pitcher-and-basin sets, beside three pearly pink dishes holding three rosy cakes of floral-scented soap.

These Jocelyn studiously ignored.

Instead, she crossed (on a pale salmon rug) to the window and pulled back the heavy amaranth covering. Here the girl received her first, and only, pleasant surprise of the day.

It was not the cherry tree framing the window in a cascade of blossoms (also pink), nor was it her view of the now nearly empty gardens and walks. No, what lifted Jocelyn's spirits was this: if she looked toward the horizon, turned her head like so and squinted her eyes like this, far in the distance she could make out a tiny patch of shoreline bordered by a bit of deep blue sea.

For the sake of that spot of blue, Jocelyn resolved that she would not set fire to her room.

At least not on her first night.

CHAPTER THREE

Ugliness and More Ugliness

Jocelyn was so intent on the patch of blue sea outside her window that she didn't hear the door open behind her. She pressed her face to the glass, squinted as hard as she could, and crossed her eyes, hoping to make out a ship. Although she had never met her father, she held high hopes for the future. Perhaps he was, at that very instant, sailing in to take her away.

Alas. No fair wind blew in her favor that day. Instead, trouble hung on the horizon.

"What is wrong with our beds?" someone whined from behind her.

Jocelyn was so startled that she turned around still cross-eyed and squinty. Two girls stood in the center of the room staring at their beds. Jocelyn's earlier, rather vigorous, investigations had left the mattresses sagging and the curtains hanging at odd angles.

"Never mind that," the taller of the two stage-whispered. "The real question is what is wrong with her face?"

The girl who asked must not have known the one about the pot calling the kettle black. She had the pinch-faced look of one perpetually waiting for a sneeze that never would arrive.

Jocelyn chose to ignore the second question. She rearranged her face into a normal expression and said, "Sorry about the beds. I was checking for spiders."

Pinch-Face squealed. "Oooh! I hate spiders! Did you catch any?"

"Unfortunately, no. They all got away. I'm Jocelyn. You must be my roommates."

The idea of spiders loose in their beds did not appear to sit well with the girls, though the shorter one quickly regained her composure. "Yes. We heard you were coming. I am Miss Priscilla Katherine-Anne Edgeworth. You may call me Prissy. This," she said motioning to Pinch-Face, "is Miss Nanette Arbuckle."

Pinch-Face smiled, adding to the frightfulness of her appearance. "You may call me Nanette. Or Nan. Or Nanette. Which do you think is better, Prissy? Perhaps Netty?"

Prissy ignored her. "If there is anything you need, you

may ask me. Anything at all. I am a particular favorite of Miss Eliza's. My mother went here when she was a girl, and my father, well, he's a very generous donor to the school."

"Good to know," Jocelyn said. "There *is* something, actually. Our room . . ."

"What about it?"

"It's very pink, isn't it?

Prissy's eyes lit up. "Don't you love it? My father paid to have it done because I wanted it. Pink is my very favorite color."

That statement told Jocelyn all she needed to know about Prissy.

"Pink is my favorite color too," Pinch-Face simpered. "I love it ever so much. I wish all the colors were pink."

In that room, they were.

Prissy narrowed her eyes and looked at Jocelyn. "And you? Do you love pink too? It's so much easier if everyone likes the same things, don't you think?"

"Yes, pink," Jocelyn replied with the barest trace of a smirk. "I find it to be every bit as lovely as the pair of you."

Pinch-Face beamed alarmingly, but Prissy frowned a little, seemingly unsure of how to take the compliment. Jocelyn continued: "How thoughtful of your father to give you such a fitting space. I can only hope that some-day *my* father will pay him a visit to properly thank him. Perhaps soon."

"Don't you mean your grandfather?" Prissy asked. "I overheard Miss Eliza saying that you lived with your grandfather because your mother—Evelina, I believe she said?—died when you were born and your father is some sort of criminal." Her smile was excessively sweet. "If I were you, I wouldn't worry too, too much about it. Dead mothers are rather fashionable these days. They lend such an attractive air of tragedy."

Pinch-Face agreed. "I wish I had one."

Jocelyn clenched her teeth but said nothing.

Prissy rolled her eyes at Pinch-Face and continued. "As for your father, Nanette's father is from the Americas, but Miss Eliza assures her that if she works very hard on her embroidery, she's nearly certain to find someone suitable to marry her. It shouldn't be so difficult for you to do the same."

"It's true." Pinch-Face nodded her head with vigor. "And, remember, you do have that dead mother. You should do tolerably well."

Jocelyn chose not to respond to their reassurances, at least not aloud. She did, however, make herself a promise. There were likely no spiders in the other girls' beds that evening, but Jocelyn resolved to remedy that as soon as possible.

One of the worst feelings in the world is being too tired to sleep. It ranks right up there with being too bored to pillage, too angry to maim, or too rich to steal. Simply dreadful.

Jocelyn's first night at school was long and difficult. She rarely slept well when she was troubled or unhappy—or hungry. True sleep eluded her, though she wasn't fully awake, either. She spent hours trapped in that twilight place between asleep and awake, where dreams are the most vivid and nonsensical, and where the Neverland draws near.

Even as she clearly felt herself lying in bed, Jocelyn dreamed she was hovering over the *Jolly Roger*. It was moored just offshore the most impossible island, where it appeared to be all four seasons at once. Warm snow drifted down, dampening the girl's hair. Below her a great squawking bird bobbed on the waves, nesting in an upturned hat.

A pirate stood on the deck of the great ship. Jocelyn was unable to clearly see his face, but in the bizarre way of dreams, she knew him to be her father. Oddly, instead of a right hand, he had an iron hook. He was locked in battle with the strangest foe—a boy dressed in a suit of skeleton leaves. Even more bewildering than the boy's youth or clothing was the fact that he was *flying*, and not with some kind of machine, or even with wings—he simply flew, as though it were as natural to him as breathing.

This soaring about seemed to be, in Jocelyn's opinion, an unfair advantage. The boy would dart in and slash with his knife, but before her father's hook or blade could cause any return damage, the cocky young thing would be floating ten feet up in the air and laughing, as if the whole thing were the greatest joke ever told.

Sounds from her bedroom intruded on Jocelyn's dream. The ocean waves were whipped up by Prissy's snoring while the mantel clock ticked loudly away, forcing the fight to keep its rhythm. It was not until dawn that Jocelyn finally drifted off into a dreamless sleep.

She woke late. Prissy and Nanette were already gone, likely on their way to the dining hall. Jocelyn was famished, and according to the clock, if she didn't hurry, she would have to stay that way a good while longer. She pulled herself out of bed and looked around for something to wear. A clean white dress was laid out and waiting. Jocelyn did like the look of a white dress. It was like a blank canvas.

Today, however, she stuck her tongue out at it and put on yesterday's traveling dress. The combination of an empty stomach, a poor night's sleep, and that hideous room had placed her in a bit of a temper. Besides, Jocelyn always felt clothes were more comfortable with a day or two's wrinkles. Somewhat cheered by happy memories brought about by the jam spots on her sleeve and streaks of dried mud on her hem, she set out for breakfast.

The dining hall was easy enough to find; Jocelyn just followed the scent of cinnamon and freshly baked pastries. Her hunger prodded her to hurry. By the time she reached a set of double doors at the end of the first-floor hallway, she was flat-out running. What a picture the girl must have made as she flung open those doors and dashed inside, skirts hiked nearly to her knees and hair flying out behind her.

Needless to say, Miss Eliza was not impressed. I wish I had been there to see the look on her old face. I hear it puckered up tighter than a frog's bottom.

All eyes, except Jocelyn's, were on the headmistress as she headed for the wild girl. Jocelyn's eyes were on the tables laden with baked goods, porridge, fruit, and cream. She couldn't wait to dig in.

"While I do appreciate you making it to breakfast on time," Miss Eliza began in an icy tone, "your entrance leaves much to be desired, as does"—she surveyed Jocelyn's rumpled clothing—"your personal appearance. I am quite certain I instructed you to dress smartly. As you have failed to follow my instructions, you shall not be dining with us. You may stand in the corner until the appropriately attired young ladies and I have finished our meal."

Jocelyn thought to argue, but a steely look in Miss

Eliza's eyes (and that puckery face, I'm sure) convinced her otherwise.

On her way to the corner, she heard Prissy tell several other girls, "Her mother is dead and her father is some kind of criminal, likely deranged. I think she might be a bit simpleminded herself. I truly do feel sorry for the poor dear—not that I'm thrilled about sharing my suite with her, but we must try to set a good example."

Pinch-Face nodded along agreeably.

Jocelyn's face burned at the injustice of it all. Still, she took her place in the corner. To keep herself from snatching pastries from a nearby plate, she imagined the punishments her father might visit upon both Prissy and Miss Eliza when he finally came for her: keelhauling, flogging with a cat-o'-nine-tails, dunking from the yardarm . . .

Absorbed as she was in these happy imaginings, the time passed more quickly than she realized. Jocelyn didn't notice when the servants began to remove empty dishes.

After her place was cleared, Miss Eliza stood to speak. "Young ladies, I am certain none of you could help but notice our newest pupil as she flew into the dining hall. However, I am confident that this morning's behavior was an anomaly and that Miss Hopewell will soon settle in, and become every bit as lovely and compliant as the rest of you. Isn't that right, Miss Hopewell?"

Jocelyn continued to stand in the corner. She was busy

picturing Miss Eliza walking the plank. There were a lot of sharks swimming around in her imagination.

"Miss Hopewell!" Miss Eliza loudly repeated.

Jocelyn jumped and looked over. "Who, me?"

"What impertinence! Of course I was speaking to you! Are you or are you not Miss Jocelyn Hopewell?"

Jocelyn clenched her fists and glared at Miss Eliza. "I am not."

Now, Miss Eliza was no novice. The woman undoubtedly knew better how to handle disturbances—though it is certain that no student had ever behaved in as rash and unruly a manner on the first morning as Jocelyn. Perhaps that was what rattled the woman into making a terrible mistake: she dared to ask, "Well then, who are you?"

Jocelyn lifted her chin and raised her eyes to Miss Eliza's. Her voice rang out clearly in the silent room. "Jocelyn Hook, only daughter and heir of Captain James Hook, the dread pirate, that's who!"

Pandemonium broke out in the dining hall. Dishes clattered to the floor. All the young ladies began to cry in terror. (If the truth be known, most of the staff joined in.) Prissy was the first to faint, which was not surprising considering she insisted on being first at everything. Then, as was their custom, the other girls followed suit, swooning one right after another like a great wave crashing on the shore. Even the formidable Miss Eliza went a bit weak in the knees at the mention of the fearful Captain Hook.

Jocelyn surveyed the carnage around her with a self-satisfied smile. Father's name always brought about such a wonderful reaction.

That smile was her undoing. The sight of it caused Miss Eliza to recover far more quickly than she might have otherwise. "Jocelyn *Hook*, is it? A dishonorable name is the only thing you will ever have from that man. Did you think he would share his hoard with you? Sail you off on an adventure? Ridiculous."

Jocelyn jerked her head back as though she had been slapped. "How dare you—"

"No, child, how dare *you*! At this school you will be known as Jocelyn *Hopewell*, and you would be wise to begin thinking of yourself that way. No new mention of that man's disgraceful deeds has reached English shores for at least five years. More to the point, if what your grandfather has told me is correct, as it undoubtedly is, even when the villain was terrorizing our seas, he never once tried to contact you. If we are fortunate, that man is dead. Yet if he does still live, one thing is certain: your father doesn't care at all about *you*."

No one had ever spoken to Jocelyn like that. She stood in stunned silence, trying to remember how to breathe. Her gaze fell upon on Prissy Edgeworth, pale from her faint but obviously thrilled at Miss Eliza's words.

Without stopping to form a plan, Jocelyn began to move. She didn't know where she would go, only that she had to get away from that ugly place with its pink walls and cruel words.

Jocelyn reached the back door and started running.

CHAPTER FOUR

Face-to-Face with Captain Hook

There are times when it feels as if retreat is the only option. For Jocelyn, this was one of those times. The girl was most definitely running away, though she had no idea where she was going, nor what she would do when she got there. All she knew was that she could not stay at that terrible school for another moment.

The morning was cold and damp. It had rained through the night and was threatening to start up again at any moment. The trail was slick with mud, and as she tried to navigate a sudden curve, Jocelyn slipped and fell. There she lay, gasping and sweating, streaked with sludge. She had never felt more tired, more hungry, or more defeated. Her eyes stung with tears that she refused to let fall, while unhappy thoughts chased one another around her mind.

Perhaps he isn't coming.

I can understand why he didn't come for me when I was younger—a ship is no place for a little child—but I'm older now. I could be such a great help to him. . . .

Perhaps he has forgotten all about me.

There she lay, quite literally wallowing in heartbreak and mud, feeling as if she couldn't possibly be any more miserable. That is, until the clouds let loose and it began to pour.

What a stroke of good luck! Without that wretched, cold rain, who knows how long the girl might have languished in her own personal slough of despond? But with it Jocelyn's physical discomfort quickly overpowered her anguish, pushing her to her feet in order to search for a place to wait out the storm.

She continued up the trail, reasoning that it must lead somewhere. Lightning flashed in the distance. If Jocelyn didn't find shelter soon, she might be forced to turn back.

Fortunately for her, it didn't come to that. Through the heavy rain, Jocelyn spied a small structure. Years before, the school had been located near where she now was. After being destroyed by a fire (one that I staunchly deny having had anything to do with), the main building was rebuilt in a location nearer the road. The old carriage house remained untouched by the flames, but it was no longer convenient for use and had been largely abandoned. It was to this building that Jocelyn came for shelter.

The heavy wooden door was swollen from the moisture in the air, causing it to stick. A brisk wind tore at Jocelyn's dress as she struggled to force her way in. Finally, she leaned her shoulder into it and shoved with all her might. With a horrible screech of its massive hinges, the door popped open and admitted the cold and dripping girl.

Inside, the room was dim, but enough light filtered through a pair of grimy windows that Jocelyn could make out her surroundings. Since it was so clearly abandoned, she incorrectly assumed that the little building would be empty. Instead, it was piled high—to the rafters in places—with items that had long outlived their usefulness and thus had been banished here...rather like an old person's house.

Or a house filled with old people.

Exploring proved to be the perfect distraction from Jocelyn's more immediate troubles. The girl quickly began thinking of the carriage house, and all the things in it, as her own. She took careful notice of what was contained in her hoard, speaking aloud an inventory of the more interesting-looking objects.

"One purple horsehair sofa with springs poking out in two—no, three—different places; a marble bust of an ugly old man, missing an ear; one grandfather clock, stopped, face cracked and missing the minute hand; several mildewed charts and maps, possibly leading to buried treasure; two matching candelabra, much of the silver leaf rubbed off; four broken dress forms; a stack of dusty blankets, don't mind if I do..."

She grabbed a couple, wrapping them around herself for warmth.

"One rusty birdcage, bright red feathers still on the bottom; and a skeleton, presumably for teaching, but one can never be sure."

Jocelyn's inventory was interrupted by a loud thump nearly directly overhead. She startled and looked up. Was there a second floor? In a shadowy corner, nearly obscured by forgotten objects, the girl spied an ancient-looking ladder disappearing into a dark, open hatch in the ceiling. Perhaps she was not alone.

Forgetting her treasures, Jocelyn carefully made her way over. She placed a hand on the ladder and stood still, listening. All was quiet above her. Even so, she couldn't shake the feeling that someone was up there. The girl began to climb to the dimly lit loft, her heart pounding, not with fear, but with the thrill of what she might discover. Sadly, upon reaching the loft and looking around, Jocelyn discovered only disappointment. Other than dust, cobwebs, and spiders, the room was empty.

Weak daylight streamed through a large round window. It was slightly ajar, the floor beneath wet from the storm. Jocelyn crossed the room to close it and stood a moment, looking out. The rain was already beginning to let up. A few brave sunbeams shone through breaks in the clouds. Overhead, the girl caught a glimpse of some great black bird soaring through the sky. She wished she could be as free.

Jocelyn was about to turn away when a sparkle caught her eye. A piece of jewelry lay on the windowsill. More treasure for her hoard?

Her fingers tingled as she held the piece up for a closer look. A heavy silver medallion hung from a dusty velvet ribbon. It was shaped like an egg, with a jeweled sea serpent on the front. In the dim light from the window, she was just able to make out an inscription on the back:

To E.H. on our wedding day.

Interesting.

Jocelyn ran her fingers over the jewels. One stuck out a bit more than the rest. She pressed it, and the pendant sprang open. It was a locket!

Inside, it held a miniature painting of a familiar-looking man. He stood at the bow of a ship, wind whipping long dark curls about his face. The look in the man's deep blue eyes was intense, fierce, and determined. Jocelyn studied it closely for several long minutes, then whispered, "Hello, Father."

CHAPTER FIVE

Jolly Roger

I'm sure you are asking yourself, "Where did the locket come from? Did it really contain a portrait of Captain Hook? Who put it in the carriage house and did he or she leave it there specifically for Jocelyn? Where can I find an honest housekeeper on the cheap?"

You may be surprised to learn that Jocelyn wasn't questioning any of these things. Being at school, she had little need to hire a housekeeper, honest or otherwise. As for the locket, she simply accepted it for what it was—a normal, average, everyday kind of miracle.

Wonderful, unexplainable things happen all the time to children, perhaps because they are such a simple-minded bunch. For instance, a child goes to bed at night and wakes in the morning to a field of snowy white. This is a miracle.

A strange dog licks instead of biting. Another miracle.

Seasons change; the earth spins round; birds defy gravity and fly. All miracles.

Compared to such wondrous things, finding your dead mother's locket bearing a picture of the father you have never met is hardly worth thinking about.

Other than feeling a mild curiosity, Jocelyn cared little where the necklace had come from. It was hers now—that was the important thing. When she tied it around her neck, she found its weight comforting somehow, as though she were suddenly less alone in the world.

She was not, however, less hungry. It had been nearly twenty-four hours since she had last eaten. Between the lack of food and sleep, the storm, and her own tangled emotions, she felt a bit weak.

Jocelyn knew that shipwrecked men set adrift on bits of debris could go at least two or three days before giving in to cannibalism, but she wasn't sure she could make it that long. She examined her options.

One: Live in the carriage house. Hope to survive on mice and beetles.

Two: Give up and die.

Three: Go back to the school.

It occurred to the girl that perhaps this whole thing was a test, set up to see if she was strong enough to handle the difficulties she might encounter if—no, *when*—she finally got to set sail on her own grand adventure. If so, she resolved to pass. Jocelyn would choose the worst of the three options.

She would go back to the school.

Mind made up, the girl reached over and plucked three or four fat spiders from a web constructed between the window and the sill. She tore the edge off her hem and made a little pouch to carry them in. "You fellows are coming with me. I can't wait until you meet your new bunkmates."

That important deed done, Jocelyn climbed down from the loft and crossed to the door. Remembering that it was difficult to open, she grabbed the handle, planted her feet, and pulled with all her might. It swung in far too easily, and Jocelyn fell to the floor, a heap of tangled petticoats and blankets.

"Hello there! What are you doing here? Are you all right?" a voice called out. Jocelyn pushed her hair away from her eyes and saw a brown-skinned, curly-haired boy, not much older than herself, kneeling next to her. His face showed a mixture of concern and amusement.

"Sorry," he said. "This door sticks—you have to shove quite hard to get it open. I didn't know anyone was on the other side. You startled me."

"*I* startled *you*? I'm not the one flinging open doors like a madman!" Jocelyn said as she struggled to right herself.

The boy offered his hand to help her up. "You're right about that. I apologize," he said with a laugh. "I'm Roger: cook's helper, undergardener, and all around errand boy here at the school. You must be Miss Eliza's new student."

Is this boy always so happy? Jocelyn wondered. *He's a regular Jolly Roger.* She stifled a giggle by checking to be sure her spiders had not been squashed when she fell.

I'm certain she made quite a picture, standing there in the weak light of the doorway: still rather soggy, streaked with mud and dust, and with cobwebs in her hair. Roger scratched his head. "You do go to school here, don't you? Did you get caught in the storm?"

"I haven't yet made up my mind."

"About whether you go to school here? Or about whether you got caught in the storm?"

"Neither of those. Yes, I go to school here, I suppose." She sighed. "And yes, I was out in the storm. I haven't yet made up my mind as to whether I like you enough to talk to you." Jocelyn pulled the door firmly closed behind her, and the pair started up the muddy path.

"Well, we're talking now," Roger said with a grin.

Jocelyn grinned back. "So we are. I'm Jocelyn Hook."

"You're not related to the fearsome Captain Hook, are you?" he asked.

Did Jocelyn detect a hint of excitement in the boy's voice? "I am," she replied cautiously. For some reason, she did not want to terrify this one. *Much*. She was enjoying walking and talking with him. "He's my father."

"Really? My father was a sailor."

"Was?"

"Yes." Roger's cheerful demeanor slipped, just a little. "My parents are both gone. My mum took sick after my dad's ship was lost. That's how I ended up here."

Jocelyn felt a growing kinship with the boy. Though she was only half an orphan in fact, she was a full one in practice. "I'm sorry about your parents."

"Me too." He cleared his throat and smiled again. "So, Captain Hook, eh? My dad used to tell the most exciting tales about him. Kept me up at night."

"My father's reputation does have that effect on people," Jocelyn said with a hint of pride. "Too afraid to sleep?"

"That wasn't it, not really. Certainly the stories gave me chills, but mostly they got me wound up. It's the whole adventure of the thing. I can't resist it."

"Do you know what?" Jocelyn asked.

"What?"

"I've made up my mind. You and I can be friends."

"Good," Roger said. "Judging from the looks of you, you'll need it. Those girls up there"—he motioned to the school growing closer with each step they took—"they could eat you alive. I don't envy you at all."

"Ugh. Don't remind me. The ones I have met are terrible, and Miss Eliza is even worse."

Jocelyn found herself confiding the whole story to her new friend. "...and that's why I was in the carriage house. I had just made up my mind to go back when you came barging in like a wild beast and knocked me over. What were you doing there anyway?"

Before answering, Roger pulled a soft, white roll from his pocket and handed it to her. Jocelyn had to stop herself from cramming the entire thing in her mouth at once.

"I go there sometimes. You know, between chores. No one ever uses it, except as a place to store odds and ends." He looked a bit embarrassed. "I like to think of it as my own secret place. You won't tell anyone, will you?"

"Tell you what," Jocelyn said around a mouthful of bread. "I won't tell if you don't"—she swallowed before continuing—"since I've decided to keep it as *my* secret place. I do aim to be a pirate, you know. This seems like a good place to start. Would you care to join my crew in exchange for carriage-house visiting privileges?"

Roger saluted with a grin. "Aye, aye, Captain. You drive a hard bargain, but I will agree to your terms."

They spit on their hands and made it official on the back steps of the school. "Well, here we are," Roger said. "Will you be all right?"

Jocelyn looked toward the door and was struck with a

desire to run away again, but having a witness to potential cowardice made it easier to be brave. She reached up and touched her necklace for strength. "I'll be fine. I'd better get it over with."

"All right, then. Cook's probably wondering where I got off to. I'll see you around." He started to leave, then turned back. "Oh, and Jocelyn?"

"Yes?"

"Good luck."

Jocelyn steeled herself for a confrontation that never came. When she entered the school, interrupting a French lesson, Miss Eliza merely waved her away, ordering a servant to accompany the girl and draw a hot bath. As Jocelyn turned to follow, Miss Eliza called after her, "Our midday meal is served at precisely half past twelve. Be sure to be on time and dress smartly, if you wish to join us. There will be no exceptions...Miss Hook."

Miss Hook? Had she heard that correctly?

Jocelyn did not quite know what to do. She had been preparing herself for battle, and the enemy had done something else entirely. What was this, a trap or surrender?

She felt a tiny, wary bit of hope. Maybe things wouldn't be so terrible at school after all.

On Jocelyn's way out, she noted Prissy's eyes, bulging with rage. Apparently, Jocelyn was not the only one surprised by Miss Eliza's reaction. Jocelyn gave Prissy her most radiant smile as she passed by, softly cradling the little bundle of spiders in her hand.

"Come on, boys," she whispered. "I hope you like pink."

CHAPTER SIX

*Wherein Jocelyn Receives a
Rudimentary Education in Warfare*

Even with Jocelyn's hopeful new outlook, she soon discovered that finishing school was no picnic. Of course, picnics are often no picnics, if you get what I'm saying. You think it's going to be nothing but fun and games, but then it's all stinging nettles, sand in your sandwiches, and who drank up the rum? No picnic indeed.

The very next morning, all occupants of the pink room were startled out of sleep by a knock at the door. "Jocelyn, you answer it," Prissy whined. "I'm not fit for receiving guests." To ensure that no one was able to peek at her with her scandalously wrinkled nightclothes and messy hair, Prissy pulled her bed curtains tight around her.

The knock sounded again. Pinch-Face looked stupidly about, then pulled her curtains closed as well.

Jocelyn stuck her tongue out at both beds, rumpled her hair up into an even rattier nest, and got up to see who was knocking. As soon as she opened the door a crack, Miss Eliza barged in. "Good morning, Miss Hook. I'm glad to see you are up. Why don't we have a seat?"

Miss Eliza strolled over to the fireplace and sat in one of the ghastly pink chairs. Jocelyn remained standing. She may have claimed a victory the day before, but the girl knew the battle was far from over. Out of the corner of her eye, she noticed Prissy's bed curtains part slightly. Whatever was to come, it would take place in front of an audience.

The headmistress was not her usual stern self. She wore a nauseating sweetness like a poorly tailored cloak. It did not suit her. "Now, Miss *Hook*"—Jocelyn noticed the way Miss Eliza emphasized her last name—"it seems we got off on the wrong foot yesterday. I blame myself, really."

"I blame you too. So we are agreed," Jocelyn replied.

Some of the old steel returned to the headmistress's voice. "Very well. Let us get straight to the point, shall we? I had assumed you capable of presenting yourself appropriately. I see now that I was wrong. As your grandfather has instructed me to spare no expense in your education, I have secured for you a personal maidservant.

She will be on hand each morning to help you wash, dress, and arrange your hair. She will then return in the evenings to help you dress for dinner." Some of the syrup returned to Miss Eliza's voice: "Won't that be lovely?"

Jocelyn's reply was cut off, which really was likely for the best. I'm not sure any of the ears in that room had ever been graced with such a string of curses as the girl was preparing to spew forth.

Jocelyn was interrupted by Prissy, frantically clawing back the curtains and tumbling out of bed. "Miss Eliza! I want a maidservant too," she said. "I know my father will pay for one. You must get one for me as well."

"Me too," Pinch-Face called from behind her bed curtains. "I'll take a maid too."

Prissy scowled and scratched at a spider bite on her arm. "Do shut up, Nanette! Miss Eliza and I are talking."

Jocelyn spoke over her, "That's fine, Pinch—er, Nanette. You can have mine. I really don't care to have one."

Prissy's face grew white and her voice went very high-pitched. "Miss Eliza, Nanette simply cannot have a maid and neither should Jocelyn. I don't mean to question your authority, but I am the only one who deserves to have a personal servant." Her tone turned threatening: "I am certain my father would agree."

Miss Eliza stood. "Miss Edgeworth, your father does not run this school, and neither do you. I do. I have made my decision and will hear no more." She glared around the room, taking in Prissy and Jocelyn—and Nanette's bed curtains. "Is that understood, ladies?"

Without waiting for a reply, she crossed to the door, opened it, and clapped her hands. A hulking figure appeared. The woman (and I use that term loosely in this case) was nearly seven feet tall and all muscle. There was nothing soft about her—even her bosom was formidable. Looking way, way up, Jocelyn noticed that the maidservant had a dark smattering of whiskers dotting her ruddy face. And that face? It did not look to be a happy one.

"Miss Hook, this is Gerta. She shall attend you from now on. I'll see you, looking smart, at breakfast."

Gerta looked down at Jocelyn and cracked her hairy knuckles. "I make you very very pretty now."

Touché, Miss Eliza. Touché.

Although Jocelyn had broken plenty of nurses, governesses, and servants in her day, Gerta proved to be the toughest. Even so, Jocelyn was sure that with time and pressure applied in just the right way, she'd be able to rid herself of this one too.

Hard as it may be to imagine, Jocelyn had a larger problem than Gerta—Prissy. That spoiled little she-devil did not like being denied. She immediately sent a message to her father, demanding that he force Miss Eliza to get her a servant of her own, and one that was better and prettier than Jocelyn's (which shouldn't have been too difficult).

Imagine Prissy's shock when her father did the unthinkable: he told her no.

It wasn't for lack of trying. Mr. Edgeworth spent the afternoon demanding, threatening, begging, and bribing, but Miss Eliza remained firm. The only student currently in need of a maidservant was Jocelyn Hook. There would be no exceptions.

To try to make up for it, the doting father promised to send his little princess several trunks filled with pretty new dresses, but she would not be consoled. It made no difference to Prissy that Jocelyn had neither asked for, nor desired, a maidservant. Jocelyn had something that she wanted. Prissy was going to make her pay.

I have faced down some horrors in my day—ferocious animals, fangs gleaming and hungry for human flesh; fierce men with murder in their eyes; my own dear mother on wash day. All were terrible to behold, but I contend that there is nothing on this earth more fearsome than a spoiled girl out for vengeance.

The next week was a grueling one for Jocelyn. She was hopeless at her lessons: her embroidery was all in knots, her sketches were "too violent," and the only French she had picked up from her tutors at home consisted of insults and swears—certainly useful under the right circumstances, but not much appreciated at finishing school. Jocelyn couldn't play an instrument, refused to sing the overly sentimental songs arranged by Miss Eliza, and was the least graceful dancer ever to waltz across a ballroom floor.

Each morning, bright and early, Gerta arrived to stuff the girl into a starched white dress and stiff shiny shoes. Entire layers of Jocelyn's skin were scrubbed away, and her hair was brushed so roughly she feared it would all be yanked out.

By the time Jocelyn made it to breakfast, feeling rather tender and raw, Prissy ensured that all the tables were full. The other girls spread out and refused to make room for Jocelyn anywhere. When she finally pushed her way into a spot, the occupants of that table would vacate it, claiming a loss of appetite. The midday meal, afternoon tea, and evening meal were no different.

Three times that week, when the young ladies put on their cloaks to go outside, Jocelyn found her pockets filled with notes:

You are ugly.

You are stoopider than anyone.

I hope you never get married, but if you do, I hope he has bad breath and is poor.

We hate you.

No one wants you here. You should go home.

If only she could have.

Miss Eliza, believing that a certain amount of societal pressure would help mold Jocelyn into a lady, pretended not to notice the cruel ways her students were behaving. If she had been a seafaring woman, she would have known: too much wind can tear a sail, too much weight can sink a vessel, and too much sun can give you the squints—then you'll have to wear spectacles.

Yet, sea or land, this is the truth: too much pressure can cause even the strongest things to break.

CHAPTER SEVEN

Sometimes Fear Is the Most Effective Weapon

Even in the face of such difficulties, Jocelyn tried to carry on, reminding herself that hardships were good training in endurance. But when she got one batch too many of hateful pocket mail, something inside her snapped.

The girls were taking their afternoon break in the garden. An early spring chill hung in the air. Jocelyn reached her hand into her pocket to warm it, when she felt papers. She drew them out and there on top was the worst one yet:

You are so horrible, even your own family did not want you.

Jocelyn did not bother to read the rest. She balled the offending papers in her fist and stood. It was time to put an end to Prissy's games.

Jocelyn focused on her target, who was holding court

on the other side of the garden. She took count of the girls surrounding Prissy. Four against one: unfair odds for sure. Unfortunate, but Jocelyn couldn't help that Prissy had so few friends around to help in the fight.

Still gripping the notes in a tight fist, Jocelyn stormed up the path. She had not gone far when she found someone blocking her way. In her rage, the girl barely registered who it was. She stepped around the obstacle and continued onward.

It pains me to admit this, but Roger was a good sight less stupid than most children. It hadn't taken him more than a minute to figure out what kind of trouble his friend was headed into. He grabbed the back of her dress and wheeled her around.

"Hello, Captain Jocelyn," he said with his usual grin. "I need to talk to you."

She slapped at his hand. "Not now, Roger. I have an appointment with Prissy over there."

Still smiling, he easily dodged out of the way. "That can wait, can't it? I need to ask you something. Something important."

Jocelyn didn't take her eyes off Prissy. "And what's that?" she asked.

"How do you feel about poisons?"

That got her attention. She pulled her gaze away from Prissy and gave Roger her full interest. "Why? Do you have some?"

"No," he admitted. "But I've got a few books about them. And some about cannibals, wild beasts, long voyages—all sorts of things." His eyes sparkled. "Naval charts and logbooks. Even a few weapons. Some old lord died and left his library to the school. Cook told me to get rid of the things that Miss Eliza didn't want, so I put them in the carriage house. Why don't you come help me unpack the boxes? Unless you want *me* to decide where everything should go."

Jocelyn took one last look at Prissy and decided her plans could wait. She allowed those dreadful notes to flutter out of her hand and scatter on the wind. "Let's go. We have new loot to attend to."

Jocelyn and Roger spent the next hour unpacking and arranging their plunder.

"Hand me those empty crates," Jocelyn commanded. "If we place them on their sides, we can use them as bookshelves."

"Aye, aye," Roger replied, stacking them in place.

She began unpacking books. "Look, *Gulliver's Travels*! Have you read it?"

"I haven't. Is it good?"

"It's fantastic! All about sea voyages to the most amazing, impossible lands. I found a copy in my mother's room and read it ragged. Heaven knows what she was doing with it."

"Do you miss her?"

"Who? My mother?" Jocelyn frowned. "I don't think so. I never knew her. And the things my grandfather tells me about her . . . she was absolutely perfect—not at all like me. I'm certain that I am not missing anything." When Jocelyn said the words, she tried to mean them, but she still felt an ache, as though there were a small, mother-shaped empty place in her heart. She tried to turn the conversation away from herself. "Do you miss yours?"

"I do. Quite a lot, to be honest. But things were worse before you arrived. I missed my mum and my dad and, well . . . just everyone. No one but Cook ever seemed to notice I was here, unless there was an order to be given."

"I rather wish people would stop noticing me. 'Jocelyn, walk like a lady.' 'Jocelyn, don't slump.' It's like everyone is looking at me, but no one truly sees me. I mean, other than you." A flush crept up her neck, and she busied herself straightening books.

"Do you know something?" Roger said, playfully nudging her with an elbow.

"What?" She nudged back, a little bit harder.

"I know you hate school, but I'm not sorry you're here."

She smiled at him, feeling a little less sorry herself. "Now, where shall we put all these maps?"

Long before their new treasure could be fully examined, Jocelyn's free time came to an end. Roger walked with her back to the school. Though the books had been an enjoyable distraction, the girl had not forgotten Prissy. When an opportunity presented itself, she captured a small green snake along the edge of the path. Jocelyn winked at Roger's curious expression and said, "I plan to teach Prissy how it feels to find nasty things in her pockets."

If you had been at Miss Eliza's school the next morning and had taken a good look at Jocelyn, you would not have noticed any redness or puffiness about her eyes. Indeed, you would have been hard-pressed to find anything amiss in either her appearance or demeanor, and why should you have? Judging by Prissy's reaction to both the snake in her pocket and a whispered threat of further retaliation, Jocelyn had been victorious.

You would never have known that Jocelyn had passed another difficult night lying awake in her too-pink bed, feeling quite deeply that not all victories are sweet—that even winning cannot remove the bitter taste of every battle.

However, even a cursory glance at Prissy would have clearly shown you that though she had decided to lay down her arms for the time being, she had not surrendered. Quite the opposite, in fact.

Prissy was just biding her time.

CHAPTER EIGHT

Dancing Lessons

Things were a little easier for Jocelyn after she acquainted Prissy with the snake. True, she did not exactly become friendly with any of the girls, but they did stop being overtly horrible. For the most part, Jocelyn went ignored by the student body—though not, unfortunately, by the headmistress.

Those first weeks dragged on, but spring did eventually turn to summer, as it often will. All the other students went home for a brief holiday, but because Jocelyn was a "special case," she was required to stay on for extra instruction. Sir Charles was a fool, but not entirely heartless. He sent gifts—new dresses, fancy writing paper, packets of embroidery needles, and other such wholly inappropriate wares—but he made it clear that his granddaughter was not to come home until she could behave like a lady. She despaired of ever leaving the school.

Unless . . .

Yes, even then Jocelyn continued to harbor secret hopes that her father might come for her, though there was still no word from him.

Many of the girls, including both Prissy and Nanette, went with their families to the popular summer holiday town of Bath. Jocelyn did not envy them—she had all the baths she could handle with Gerta. The poor girl's skin was in a constant state of rawness from the rough scrubbing it received twice a day. Jocelyn tried everything she could think of to scare her servant off, but to no avail. The woman was absolutely imperturbable.

Between Gerta's violent attentions and Miss Eliza's personal instruction in "the fine arts of womanhood," Jocelyn was nearly completely miserable. It was only her friendship with Roger that kept her from becoming absolutely wretched. If I am not mistaken on this point (and I am rarely mistaken), it was Roger's idea that allowed Jocelyn to be a bit more successful at finishing school, yet still remain herself.

They were whiling away another lazy afternoon by hiding in the carriage house. The summer air was much cooler inside the old building, making it an excellent place to stow away. Roger hid there from Cook, who became increasingly bad-tempered as the thermometer rose, and Jocelyn from Miss Eliza, who was determined to teach her errant pupil to walk like a lady before the end of the summer: "No, no, no, no, child. We don't stomp and we don't slouch. We glide, like a swan. Now be a swan. . . ."

It's no wonder the pair crept away as often as they could. They spent many hours holed up together plotting and preparing for future adventures. In this regard, the late Lord Wellesley's library proved to be quite helpful, allowing them to live a lifetime of daring deeds in paper and ink. A set of wooden practice swords afforded them a chance to learn rudimentary swordsmanship, though the pair turned up their noses at their deceased benefactor's antique flintlock pistol, feeling that firearms were inelegant. Instead, Roger taught Jocelyn how to throw a punch and she taught him how to spit—not just any old sputum spewing, mind you, but spitting with purpose and feeling. Spiteful spitting.

I am no novice spitter myself, having once hit a mermaid squarely in the eye from the deck of a fast-moving clipper, but I have to admit, that girl's saliva slinging could put even me to shame.

But I digress. We were talking about Roger and his idea.

Jocelyn sprawled upside down on the horsehair sofa, her legs slung over the back, her head hanging off the edge of the seat cushions. She fingered her necklace as she explained to Roger how terrible it felt to be first scrubbed to the bone, then imprisoned all morning for lessons. "I absolutely hate it. She's forcing me to do all these things that I have no interest in whatsoever. It makes me want to throw something: my books, the tea tray, a screaming fit. The worst part is I have no choice. If I don't perform at my lessons, I'll never get to go home, not even for a visit. But if I do, they all win. I'll become nothing more than a pretty little puppet." She slapped the sofa cushion, sending up a cloud of dust. "I'd rather die."

Roger was in the corner, attacking a dress form with one of the wooden swords. From Jocelyn's upside-down vantage point, it looked as if her friend were fighting on the ceiling. It reminded her a little of that odd dream about her father and the flying boy.

He sat on the floor near her, leaning against the couch, and put his sword down. "Don't die," he said. "What fun would that be? For me, I mean."

She reached over and gave him a little shove. "This is serious."

"Oh yes. Serious. I can tell." He arranged his face into mock gravity. "Do you dance?"

"What? Why?"

"Only wondering. Do you?"

"Yes," she said, frowning. "Dancing is one of the worst parts. Miss Eliza makes me partner with Gerta so that she can be free to 'observe my form.' Gerta smells like cabbage soup and I am constantly tripping over her feet. Am I to be blamed that they stick out so far?"

"Absolutely not."

"Tell that to her. She punishes me for every misstep when it's time to dress for dinner." Jocelyn touched the tip of her nose, rubbed raw from scrubbing. "And then there's Miss Eliza, constantly reminding me that I'll need to work extra hard if I want to keep from embarrassing myself in front of the 'young gentlemen' she has invited to this year's holiday ball. As though I'd want to dance with any sweaty-palmed, disgusting boy. No offense."

"None taken. I'm sure it is no more than I would want to dance with some clumsy girl." He winked at her. "No offense."

Jocelyn thumped him on the head with a sofa pillow. He pulled it out of her hands and placed it behind his back. "Thank you. That's far more comfortable."

Jocelyn laughed. "Roger, why did you ask about dancing?"

"Well," he replied, "the way I see it is this: When it comes to your lessons, Miss Eliza pipes and you have to dance—but who is to say you can't choose your own steps?"

★ ★ ★

Jocelyn mulled over Roger's words for a day or two. The girl didn't seem to have much power over her own life, but it was still hers. If she was going to be forced to learn a slew of useless things, she wanted to be sure to do it her own way.

She made up her mind to try, starting with Gerta. It occurred to Jocelyn that the only way to finally be rid of her burly maidservant was to prove that she no longer needed one. Though it pained her to have to choose a clean dress and fresh underclothes every single day, to at least try to run a comb through her hair, and to wash all the visible parts of her body, it proved to be far less painful that the torment Gerta inflicted with her rough washcloths and wire-bristle brush.

To Jocelyn's immense relief, Gerta was soon sent packing. Once she was no longer suffering under the ministrations of that torturous maidservant, Jocelyn set her attentions to her lessons. She tried to make a game of finding ways to satisfy Miss Eliza without feeling like she was selling her own soul. It was a delicate balancing act, but I think she managed all right. One unexpected benefit was this: the more politely Jocelyn behaved, the less scrutiny Miss Eliza gave her. It became even easier to slip off and spend her free time with Roger.

When the rest of the students returned from summer holiday, they found an exceedingly more accomplished Miss Hook than the one they had left. On the first day of term, during the Art of Needlework, Miss Eliza pointed out how much Jocelyn's embroidery had improved. After just a few weeks, the girl's stitches could truthfully be described as dainty. The headmistress's only criticism was that instead of floral patterns, Jocelyn created seat covers and pincushions decorated with tiny skull-and-crossbones patterns or unusual torture devices.

Fine ladies from the local village confessed to being quite charmed by Jocelyn's singing in the school's fall talent exhibition. They complimented Miss Eliza on her pupil's clear, high voice, sweet enough to touch the stoutest heart—even if the young lady's song choice, "It's All for Me Grog, Me Jolly, Jolly Grog," did raise a few eyebrows.

Jocelyn also made great strides with her mastery of French. Miss Eliza was most certainly pleased, though I imagine she would have preferred that Jocelyn memorize phrases such as *Mais oui, j'ai en effet trouvé le camembert délicieux* ("Why yes, I did find the Camembert delicious") instead of *Pardonnez-moi, mais il semble que j'ai coincé ma fourchette à poisson dans votre oeil* ("Pardon me, but it seems that I have lodged my fish fork in your eye"). Still, it could not be denied that progress was being made.

There is no doubt that Jocelyn chose her steps quite well, though she did tire of the dance. As weeks turned to months, the girl felt as if the proverbial clock would never strike twelve and bring an end to the ball. Yet how was she to know that one day, not far distant, instead of wishing for the clock to speed up, Jocelyn would desperately hope for a way to stop its dreadful ticking?

CHAPTER NINE

A Taste of Adventure,
Inspired by Ferdinand Magellan

There is nothing more difficult than trying to force yourself to sleep on those long, long nights when your mind refuses to be quieted. Unless, of course, you count swimming the English Channel while wearing iron underpants. Or training octopi to darn socks. Or winning at backgammon against my cousin Bartimus.

Bartimus is very good at backgammon.

All right, there are many things more difficult than trying to force yourself to fall asleep on those long, long nights when your mind refuses to be quieted, but that fact does not make the hours pass any more quickly.

On the night before Jocelyn's thirteenth birthday she found herself, once again, caught in the grip of insomnia.

She tossed and turned in her too-pink bed, too excited to sleep.

After lunch that day, Jocelyn had slipped off to the carriage house, where she and Roger spent the afternoon reading a thrilling history of Ferdinand Magellan. His was a wonderful tale full of shipwrecks, exploring uncharted lands, mutiny, marooning, even murder. In the end, Captain Magellan was stabbed to death by angry natives wielding bamboo spears. His body was never recovered.

Jocelyn's heart pounded with longing for such a thrilling life, though she could do without the murdered-by-stabbing bit. However, if that was the price required, she was sure she'd gladly pay it, at least twice. Finally, unable to stand it any longer, the girl pulled back her bed curtains and crept across the room. If she could catch a glimpse of the sea from her window, perhaps it would calm her enough to drop off to sleep.

At least that was the lie that she told herself. In truth, Jocelyn knew it was too dark to make out anything of the distant waves—unless there were lights on the water. *The kind of lights that might be on her father's ship.*

She held her breath to keep from fogging the glass and stared as hard as she could in the right direction, but saw nothing. The only lights outside her window were stars.

No matter. So, her father wasn't coming tonight. She still must do something; the thought of returning to bed was unbearable. Jocelyn's whole soul filled with mutinous desire. The window was already open a little. She eased the sash up the rest of the way, grabbed a limb of the cherry tree, and swung herself out. From there it was no difficult feat to climb down.

When her slippered feet touched the dewy grass, the girl felt, for the first time in months, completely free. The night wrapped about her, alive and mysterious. A full moon shone, illuminating the garden. A warm breeze ruffled Jocelyn's hair. She closed her eyes and pretended to be a great explorer, standing on a foreign shore.

Her imaginings were interrupted by the sharp crack of a twig snapping. Something was moving through the nearby shrubbery. Jocelyn had an abrupt vision of Magellan, torn and bleeding at the edge of a lonely sea. She scanned her surroundings for a weapon—a stick, a rock, anything—but the ground was bare.

More rustling came from the thick hedgerow. There was definitely something, or someone, moving her way. In desperation, Jocelyn pulled off one of her slippers and held it out in front of her.

"Who's there?" she whispered.

No answer came.

"I know someone is there," she said. "Be warned, I am heavily armed."

All was still. She moved toward the shrubbery, wielding her slipper. There were more rustling sounds; then something burst from the bushes and ran straight for her. Jocelyn jumped and threw her weapon at it.

It was only a cat. A great ugly cat, but still, nothing but a cat. Her slipper connected solidly with its body—though sadly, being only cloth, it did no damage. (Have I mentioned I do not care for cats?)

The ugly beast yowled and shot into the night. Jocelyn tried to catch her breath. Once her heart slowed to a near normal pace, she crossed to retrieve her slipper. As she stooped to pick it up, she heard a whisper: "Nice arm."

The girl whirled around, slipper once again at the ready—only to find Roger, doubled over with silent laughter. "Don't hurt me," he gasped. "I'm unarmed."

Jocelyn hurled her slipper, smacking him in the forehead.

Roger fell to his knees and laughed even harder. "I'm s-s-s-sorry." He could hardly speak. "It's ju-just that . . . seeing you there . . . with your sl-sl-slipper at the ready . . ." That was all he could get out.

Jocelyn tried to be angry, but Roger's laughter was infectious. She couldn't help but join in. "What about you?" she asked. "Incapacitated by hilarity? Perhaps that was my plan all along."

Roger took a shuddering breath and tried to regain control. "It was a rousing success," he said. "I may laugh myself to death. Such dangerous footwear . . ." He lost himself to laughter again.

The children lay side by side in the grass, giggling as quietly as they could manage. The lateness of the hour made everything seem far more humorous than it otherwise would have been. Their sides ached and tears burned their eyes. Every time one managed to calm down, the other started up again.

After what felt like a very long time, Jocelyn finally recovered her wits enough to whisper, "What are you doing out here?"

"Magellan," Roger replied. "You?"

"The same. There was no way I could stay in bed."

They lay there, sprawled on the lawn, in companionable silence for a time. "You know," Jocelyn said, "tomorrow is my birthday."

"Is it? I'd forgotten."

"Oh. You did? Well, that's no matter. It's not that important, really. It's merely..."

Roger propped himself up on an elbow and looked intently at Jocelyn. "Merely what?"

"I suppose it's that I'll be thirteen tomorrow. I've been stuck here for nearly a year, and ... I don't know. Sometimes I can hardly stand it. You know, that feeling—"

"That there is some great adventure out there, just waiting to be had?" Roger interrupted.

"Precisely. Uncharted seas, exotic ports of call, jungles filled with wild beasts—"

"Man-eating plants and cannibals. Things we can only dream of . . . I know."

"Oh, Roger, I've read all the books we have. Many of them more than once. I've learned to fight. I'm ready. But instead of doing heroic deeds, I'm stuck here. Making pincushions."

"The world does need pincushions."

"And you need another slipper thrown at you."

He smiled his special, just-for-Jocelyn smile. "You'll have your chance one day, Jocelyn. We both will. I'm sure of it." Roger lay back on the grass again and they fell quiet, gazing at the stars. "Look up there," he said, pointing. "See that star? The bright one, second to the right of the Big Dipper? That's the North Star. One day, you'll find yourself following it into a great adventure."

Jocelyn fixed the star firmly in her memory.

"Unless, of course, your adventure begins in the daytime," Roger went on. "In that case, you'll be out of luck."

Jocelyn giggled and nudged her friend with her elbow. "You're horrible."

"I know. So are you. And Jocelyn?"

"What?"

"Did you really think I could forget your birthday?" He sat up and reached into his pocket. "I was going to wait until tomorrow, but . . ." He dropped something small and metallic into her outstretched hand.

Jocelyn sat up to get a better look at it. By the light of the moon, she recognized a small brass compass.

"That isn't your actual present," Roger said. "It's more of a loan. I do want it back one day. It was my dad's—my mum gave it to me before she died—but I thought you might like to hold on to it for a while. That way, you won't lose your direction, even if you can't see the stars."

"It's beautiful. Thank you. I'll take good care of it."

"Now, for your actual present." He looked right into Jocelyn's eyes. "I don't have much, but I can give you a birthday promise. One day, hopefully soon, we'll use that compass together and set sail for a great adventure. I don't know when or how, but I am certain we will. You have my word on that."

The night was unseasonably warm and scented with lilacs. Crickets played their minuscule violins. Up above, those wicked, wicked stars twinkled down on a boy and a girl sitting ever so close together, alone in the dark.

Jocelyn leaned toward Roger, parted her lips, and—

You know, if they had been a few years older and more interested in that sort of thing, this is the part where they might have kissed. I'm so glad they didn't. It would have ruined the whole story.

As it was, Jocelyn leaned toward Roger, parted her lips, said, "Thanks," and then punched him on the arm.

He said, "You're welcome," and pulled her hair.

After that she was forced to throw her slipper again.

Later, as she climbed the tree to her window, Jocelyn replayed their little adventure in her mind. She was so glad to have Roger as her friend. How terrible it would have been at school without him.

Preoccupied as she was by such happy thoughts, Jocelyn didn't notice that her room was far too quiet. Prissy's usual snoring was missing.

CHAPTER TEN

Consequences

Most things are obvious in hindsight. That mysterious stranger was not attempting to do you harm; he only wanted to return your dropped wallet. Your parents were not plotting your demise; they were planning a surprise party. The surprise party turned out to be a ruse and your parents were planning your demise after all. Without the benefit of hindsight, innocent things seem wicked. Nefarious things seem absolutely ordinary. Illumination comes only after the fact.

Perhaps this is why Jocelyn felt unconcerned when Roger was nowhere to be found the next morning. She knew he would turn up eventually; it was her birthday, after all. Yet as afternoon wore into evening with no word from her friend, Jocelyn couldn't help but feel a little wounded.

I know he gave me my gift last night, but it would have been nice to see him today, she thought as she prepared herself for dinner.

Prissy and Nanette were on the other side of the room, talking about boys. "... and my papa said that in a year or two he'd bring me to Boston for a big party so I can meet lots of eligible young men. In the Americas, they call that a coming-out party."

If I saw that pinched-up face coming out, I'd shove it back in, Jocelyn thought. *Roger would laugh if I told him that. Where is he?*

The window was open, bringing into the room a faint scent of lilac blossoms. Outside, Jocelyn could hear the gardener working. From the noise he was making, it sounded like the back garden was about to get quite a renovating. Perhaps that was where Roger had been all day.

Even so, it was her birthday.

In a streak of rebellion, Jocelyn decided not to change her dress for dinner. So what if the seat was slightly grass-stained? She'd be sitting on it; who would notice?

Her revolt was interrupted by Miss Eliza knocking at the door.

Jocelyn sighed and reached for a clean dress. "I was getting ready to change, Miss Eliza."

"No need for that just now, Miss Hook. I have come to have a word with you. Miss Edgeworth, Miss Arbuckle, please excuse us."

Prissy gave Jocelyn a look of gloating satisfaction as she and Nanette left the room.

This must be bad, thought Jocelyn. *Whatever it is, Prissy knows about it. I hope they are not bringing Gerta back.*

"Miss Hook," the headmistress began, "please sit. I have something rather delicate to discuss with you." Strange—Miss Eliza was blushing a bit. Jocelyn sat, wondering what could possibly be the cause.

"When one starts to get older..." The headmistress cleared her throat. "Quite often, girls of your age may begin to go through certain emotional and physical changes.... Rather, you are getting to be old enough where it is, ah, perfectly natural... Oh dear." Miss Eliza pressed her lips together and drew a deep nasal breath. "You may find yourself having new and exciting feelings.... What I mean to say is, one does begin to notice members of the opposite..." She trailed off and looked at Jocelyn hopefully. "Do you see what I mean, Miss Hook?"

"Er...no."

"'Er...no' is not an appropriate—oh, never mind about that. I'll get right to the point. Is this yours?" She held up a dirty blue bedroom slipper. In the excitement of the night before, Jocelyn hadn't realized that it was missing. The gardener must have found it outside when he started work.

Speaking of which, it was getting pretty noisy outside.

"What is he doing back there?" Jocelyn wondered aloud. "Chopping wood?"

"What is happening outside this room is none of your immediate concern, Miss Hook. I asked you a question."

"Oh, yes, my slipper. Thank you for returning it. Is that all you wanted to talk about?"

"Then it *is* yours." Some of the color drained away from Miss Eliza's face. "I had hoped Miss Edgeworth to be mistaken. The situation could prove to be very bad, both for you and for my school. If word of the scandal gets out..." Miss Eliza straightened herself up. "Well, we will just have to make certain that it does not."

"Miss Eliza," Jocelyn asked, "why would Prissy care about me losing my slipper? It's not as if it was a gift from my fairy godmother. What is so scandalous about it?"

"This is not some fairy tale, Miss Hook. This is serious. Miss Edgeworth reported to me that you were out of bed last night. In fact, not only that you were out of bed, but that you climbed out your window and into the back gardens, where you were seen cavorting with the kitchen boy. Your slipper was recovered there this morning."

"There was no 'cavorting' going on. But yes, I couldn't sleep and—*what* is going on back there?" Jocelyn looked to the window in time to see the cherry tree fall. She leaped to her feet, but Miss Eliza grabbed her by the wrist and pulled her back into her chair.

"Miss Hook, you do not seem to grasp the gravity of the situation. You were out, late at night, unchaperoned, and in the company of a boy not only well below your station but also completely unsuitable in *every* imaginable way. Something like this could have serious repercussions in regards to your future prospects."

Jocelyn angrily rubbed her wrist. "Something like what?"

"A young woman of your social position," Miss Eliza stammered, "choosing a . . . a . . . *kitchen boy* for a paramour—"

"A para-what?"

"A beau. A suitor. A conquest. Call him whatever you like, this boy is not suitable for you."

A look of horror came over Jocelyn's face. Now it was her turn to stammer. "You thought that Roger and I . . . that we were . . . that he was my . . . That is disgusting! Roger is only my—"

"It does not matter what he *was*. From this point on he *is* nothing. Your grandfather has plans for you and they do not include poor, uneducated serving boys."

Blood pounded in Jocelyn's head, and two small red spots lit up her blue eyes. She stood and glared down at Miss Eliza. "Those are *his* plans, not mine. I choose my own friends."

Miss Eliza's face softened. "Miss Hook—Jocelyn—please sit down." The use of her given name brought Jocelyn up short. "I can understand how you must be feeling. But as women, our choices are limited. Your grandfather will not live forever. It is unlikely that he has shared the details of his estate with you, but perhaps if I do, it will help you to understand." Miss Eliza paused and looked questioningly at Jocelyn.

"Well, go on," the girl said, still standing.

"Your grandfather's wealth and property are entailed. This means that they must go to a male heir. As Sir Charles hasn't any sons to inherit, all of it—his money, his holdings, everything he owns—will revert back to his closest male relation. This relative may take pity and provide a small pension for you to live off, but it is unlikely he would do more. Your grandfather has always known that your only hope for a secure future is to marry well." She stared, unblinking, into Jocelyn's eyes. "Marrying well will be difficult to do if there are questions about your conduct."

This was news to Jocelyn. A heavy feeling settled in her stomach. That was the reason her grandfather placed such high importance on turning her into a lady? It occurred to the girl with abrupt finality that she would never be able to change his mind.

"Here is what we are going to do," Miss Eliza continued. "Though it pains me to resort to this, I'm fairly certain I will be able to keep Miss Edgeworth from speaking of last night's incident if I provide her with a personal servant or two.

"The kitchen boy has been dismissed, though I did make other arrangements for him. He was escorted from the premises this morning and given strict instructions that should he speak even one word about you, or try to contact you in any way, I shall go straight to the magistrate and have him shipped off to the Americas like a criminal."

Jocelyn could not believe what she was hearing. She tried to tell herself it was nothing more than an awful nightmare, but even pinching her wrist as hard as she could didn't awaken her.

"As for you, since you have begun to show an interest in young men, I am arranging for you to have a short visit home to London. I am certain Sir Charles will be in complete agreement when he receives my letter explaining how eager you are to mingle with the right sort of families. I believe you have already made the acquaintance of Ambrose Trottington? He is only one of many suitable boys near your age."

Jocelyn was speechless. She stood frozen, quaking with emotion.

"Don't get overly excited. This is simply an opportunity for the young gentlemen to meet you and see what a fine young lady you are becoming. You are still a bit young for romance. I know it can feel like a long time to wait, but we'll lay the groundwork now, and perhaps in a year or two you will be ready to begin a formal courtship.

"I will call for a carriage early in the morning. You are to remain here for the duration of the night. As for dinner, I will have a tray sent up when the chambermaid comes to take your measurements."

Jocelyn's mind caught on that last part. "My measurements? What for?"

Miss Eliza smiled for the first time since she entered the room. "Why Miss Hook, I believe you are now ready for more grown-up attire. You must be measured for new dresses." She gave Jocelyn an appraising look. "And, I think...yes, a set of corsets."

CHAPTER ELEVEN

The Neverland Comes to Finishing School

When Miss Eliza opened the door to leave, an eavesdropping Prissy fell into the room, her face glowing with malicious glee. Miss Eliza sniffed disapprovingly, but likely feeling that she had enough to handle with Jocelyn's situation, she kept her tongue and swept from the room.

Prissy's tongue, however, would not be kept. "I knew you and that dirty servant boy were up to something, always disappearing together during free time. I could have told Miss Eliza about it months ago, but I had a feeling if I waited, you'd do something really awful. Did you get thrown out of school?" She didn't wait for Jocelyn to answer. "Really, Jocelyn, I would have never guessed you could stoop so low. It must be in your blood. I mean, look at the kind of man your mother—"

And that's as far as she got.

"Don't you ever, ever talk about my mother, you stupid cow!" Jocelyn hissed. Then, to make sure that her point was received, she drew back and gave that horrible girl a long-overdue knuckle punch to the eye. Prissy covered her face with her hands and fell to the floor, screaming.

Rather a bit more loudly than was called for, I might add.

"And keep your mouth shut about Roger as well," Jocelyn muttered as she stepped over her. Prissy's shrieks were bound to bring the headmistress and more trouble. For the second time since her arrival at Miss Eliza Crumb-Biddlecomb's Finishing School for Young Ladies, Jocelyn ran.

Jocelyn didn't have time to formulate much of a plan. She had a few vague notions of escape, perhaps by stowing away on a ship somehow, but nothing concrete.

To be honest, even then she still held out hope her father would come for her. Sadly, she would soon find more disappointment. Jocelyn was about to discover that the great Captain Hook would never sail her off on a great adventure.

Much like the first time she considered running away from school, the girl made her way to the carriage house.

She cradled a small hope that Roger would be there, waiting. Even if he wasn't, she would need supplies, and there were plenty of things in her hoard that could be useful. However, once she got to the carriage house, Jocelyn's drive left her.

It was clear that Roger had not been there since the day before. His favorite book (*Impress Your Friends, Confound Your Enemies: 1001 Poisonous Jungle Plants and How to Use Them*) lay facedown on the sofa where he had left it when Magellan's history had beguiled him away. Jocelyn sank down next to the book.

She relied so much on Roger's friendship. What would she do without him? Jocelyn wondered if he was angry with her for his unfair dismissal. She reached over, picked up the book, and tore out a page. After digging in the couch cushions, she unearthed a lead pencil.

Dear Roger, she began, right between the entries for cowhage (causes blindness) and devil's apple (causes delirium and hallucinations), *I'm sorry...*

Her pencil paused on the page. Sorry for what, exactly?

That she'd gotten him dismissed?

That she hadn't appreciated him more?

That he was gone?

All of that and more, but she didn't know how to say it. Jocelyn left the note as it was, signing at the bottom of the page *From your friend, Jocelyn.* She intended to leave it on the arm of the sofa, where Roger would be sure to find it if he ever returned.

This would have been an excellent time for the girl to form a plan for the future, but she couldn't seem to wrap her mind around the magnitude of her problem. Where would she go? What would she do? At the moment, all the energy Jocelyn had left was used up wrapping herself in a blanket and turning her face to the window. She felt as if she had spent her entire life looking through panes of glass, waiting for something exciting to happen, but nothing ever did.

Jocelyn lay on the sofa for quite some time—unwilling even to move in her misery. She knew that Miss Eliza would have people searching for her, but she couldn't bring herself to care. The sky outside grew dark. From her vantage point on the couch, the girl had a perfect view of the North Star. She closed her eyes and made a wish.

I do not desire to deceive you—about stars, anyway. The North Star is not a wishing star. In the history of the world, no wishes made on the North Star have ever come true. Unless, that is, it also happened to be the wisher's birthday.

"I wish for an extraordinary adventure, far away from this place, and I wish one for Roger, too, wherever he is."

Nothing happened.

At least, not right away, but if you will quit squirming about and be patient you will see that most things in life, wishes included, do not have immediate results.

Believing her wish to have been wasted, Jocelyn took matters into her own hands. She would not wait for some sort of magic to whisk her away from her problems. If they were to be solved, she must do it on her own. Outside, she could hear her name being called. It was faint but distinct: the head gardener was searching for her. She would not let him find her helplessly huddled in a blanket.

Jocelyn got up, unearthed a satchel from her hoard, and filled it with a moth-eaten nightgown and a few books. What more could a girl need? With her mother's necklace around her neck and Roger's compass in her pocket, she was ready to go. It didn't really matter where, as long as she left on her own terms.

Jocelyn had taken two steps toward the door when a noise at the window caused her to turn back. Something large and dark filled the frame. Something inhuman.

Its clawed talon scraped at the glass, struggling to raise the sash. Whatever the creature was, it wanted in. Jocelyn felt so absolutely ready for something to happen, it didn't occur to her to be frightened—though she did take up one of the wooden swords, to be on the safe side. She crossed to the window and threw it wide, coming face-to-face with the strangest being she had ever seen.

In form and feather the creature appeared to be a crow, but not at all like any Jocelyn had encountered before. It was immense, easily twice the girl's size, and much darker than a garden-variety crow—as though no light dared sully its sleek plumes. The great bird ducked its head and pushed through the opening, filling the room with shadow and inky black. Jocelyn backed up and raised her weapon, such as it was. How she wished she were holding a blade of steel instead of wood.

In case you are wondering, *that* wish did not come true.

It advanced upon her. Jocelyn swung her sword with all her might, but the creature was ready, easily avoiding her blow. With a flap of its dark wings, it rushed the girl, knocking her flat. Placing a taloned foot on her chest, the crow pinned her to the floor. Jocelyn struggled but could not get up.

"Get off me, you ridiculous dodo! What do you want?" she shouted.

Bending its head, the bird turned a shiny black eye on the girl. Jocelyn did not particularly enjoy its strangely intelligent appraisal. She broke contact, looking away. Her gaze fell upon a leather pouch tied to the creature's leg. The bird bent, untied the cord with its beak, and withdrew a packet of papers. These it tucked up under a wing; then it addressed the girl with a surprisingly mild voice. "Your name, please?"

Jocelyn's eyes widened. "You can speak?"

"Considerably better than any dodo." The bird removed its foot from her chest and allowed Jocelyn to stand. "Now. Your name? You are Jocelyn Hook, are you not?"

She nodded.

"Very good. I am Edgar Allan of Edgar Allan's Mainland Courier Service. Please sign here for your letter." He removed a form from the bundle of papers under his wing and pushed it toward the girl, indicating with his beak where she should sign. Jocelyn scribbled her name on the line.

"Thank you," he said, presenting her with the rest of the packet. "I will wait here for your response."

"My response to what?"

Edgar motioned to the papers he had given her, then turned away and began to preen his feathers.

The girl's fingers shook as she unfolded the packet. Whatever happened next would most definitely be extraordinary. She smoothed the papers, pushed back an unruly lock of hair, and bent her head to examine the message.

Jocelyn held, at long last, a letter from her father.

CHAPTER TWELVE

A Voice from Beyond the Horizon

Jocelyn swallowed, her mouth suddenly dry. The letter quivered in her trembling hands. Steadying herself, she began to decipher the bold strokes of thick, black ink covering the page.

> Dear Female Offspring,
> Since you are now reading this epistle, the thing I fear has most assuredly happened. I am dead.

Jocelyn stared with shock at the page. She turned to Edgar, who nodded his head and motioned for her to continue.

Please do not shed many tears for me, although a few would be nice. Even the most wicked and sinister man, such as myself, takes comfort in the thought that someone will mourn his passing.

I have lived a good life. For many years I have ransacked, plundered, and slashed with both blade and hook. Few have lived a more fulfilling existence.

I am feared by all men, yet I fear none. Indeed, I fear no man or boy—especially no boy!

Yet herein lies my only shame. Call this my last confession: I am afraid of something. Indeed, if the truth be told, I am terrified.

A cold-blooded nightmare stalks my every waking minute. I am haunted by rows of razor-sharp teeth and the ticking of a fiendish timepiece.

Yes, it is true! I live in fear of the dreadful crocodile who feasted first upon that confounded clock and then upon my right hand. On that terrible day, I stared the beast in its terrible eye and felt its power. It seemed to take my measure as a man, and, to my eternal disgrace, I was found lacking.

From that time to this, I have lived in shame.

And yet the horror grows! Earlier this evening, while resting in my quarters, I beheld a vision of my own death at the beast's sharp jaws. Smee tries to comfort me. He tells me I am simply the victim of a bad dream, but he is wholly incorrect.

I am Captain James Hook! I am no victim; I create them!

I do not have bad dreams; I inspire them!

No, this was something else: a warning of my ultimate demise. Now a grim reptilian specter of death is my truest companion.

It is my hope that penning these words will offer me some relief. Perhaps I will yet become the conqueror. I will master my fear and blast the infernal creature to hell!

And yet, if you are reading this, my victory was not to be. The crocodile has sent me to my doom. My heart has stopped, but the beast's dreadful ticktock continues.

Oh, the injustice!

You are my only heir. As such, you must avenge my death. I lay this charge upon you: Come to the Neverland. Hunt the beast and destroy it in my name.

I have no doubt you will fail, for you are practically an infant, and a girl besides. However, as my only progeny, you must try. With my blood in your veins, you may yet overcome these weaknesses and bring me victory.

Floreat Etona!

J̃s. Hook

P.S. You must consider this quest your inheritance, along with a few personal effects and a small bag of coins left with my bo'sun, Mr. Smee. I may not be able to take my riches into the afterlife, but that is no reason to give them away.

Jocelyn read and reread the words on the page. She couldn't seem to stop herself. She felt that were she to finish the letter and lay it aside, only then could it be true. Captain James Hook might not have been a good father, but he was the only one she had. Once she set the paper down, their connection would be broken. He would never come for her; she would truly be an orphan.

After several minutes, Edgar gently grasped the letter in his beak, pulled it from her shaking hands, and set it beside her. That was when the tears came, but as her father had requested, Jocelyn did not shed many for him. Most of the tears were for herself.

Now let us show some respect and observe a moment of silence.

Done so soon?
I should have known it wouldn't last.

No one cries forever. Before much time had passed, Jocelyn dried her eyes and began to think. When she'd wished for adventure, this wasn't what she had in mind, but wishes are heartless. They care little for nuances.

The girl's head spun and her heart thumped in a

strange rhythm. It was beating so loudly she could almost hear it. Instead of *ba-boom, ba-boom, ba-boom,* it went *tick-tock, tick-tock, tick-tock.* With a start she realized the sound was not coming from within her; it came from elsewhere in the room.

I believe I mentioned earlier an old grandfather clock among the castoffs in the carriage house? Presumably, Miss Eliza had banished it because it had stopped running. Perhaps it was merely a coincidence, only a freak chance—or perhaps, like a grandfather who enjoys tricking small children into believing noses can be stolen, the clock took sinister delight in Jocelyn's pain. Whatever the reason, it chose that instant to break its long silence.

tick-tock, tick-tock . . .

Jocelyn fingered the locket that hung from her neck. She closed her eyes and imagined the crocodile.

tick

A fierce battle between man and boy rages above the sea. The hungry crocodile surfaces from the deep, tasting the water for blood.

tock

The boy's blade flashes, slicing off a treat for the waiting beast. Without hesitation the crocodile snaps up its meal, swallowing it whole.

tick

That one small morsel awakens an irrepressible hunger deep within the creature: a hunger that cannot be satisfied until the rest of Captain Hook joins his hand in the belly of the crocodile.

tock

Man and beast lock eyes. The captain's fate is sealed.

The Neverland's crocodile not only killed Captain Hook; it stole from her:

Her father.

Her dreams.

Her future.

TICKTOCKTICKTOCKTICKTOCK

Jocelyn's eyes flew open, the ticking sound loud and terrible in her ears. She grabbed her wooden sword and hurled it with all her strength. It connected with the clock's face, creating a wonderful crash. Broken glass, springs, and gears rained down, littering the carriage house floor. Silence filled the room. Jocelyn dusted her hands, shouldered her bag, and nodded at Edgar.

The crocodile deserved to be punished for its crimes. The penalty would be death.

CHAPTER THIRTEEN

*In Which Our Heroine Receives Her
First Taste of Government Bureaucracy
(and Does Not Care for It)*

Early the next morning, when Jocelyn caught her first glimpse of the Neverland's shores, I am ashamed to report that she...well, she *squealed*. Just a little, mind you, but it was there. Thankfully, Jocelyn was not a girl prone to such banality. And in her defense, the sight below was nothing short of astonishing. I think we can forgive her this once.

The girl sat suspended in a woven hammocklike sling, useful for passengers or packages, that Edgar carried in his powerful claws. This perch gave her a panoramic view of the entire Neverland. For such a small landmass, it presented an incredible amount of variety: beaches and mountains, jungles and deserts, fields of bloodthirsty wildflowers, half-hidden coves, and several villages. An enormous volcano grew from the center of the island, sending up the most intricate series of smoke signals. If Jocelyn could have read them, she'd have seen that the Neverland was welcoming her; indeed, it was even showing off a bit.

On the south side of the island that day (I say that day, for the Neverland changes itself around as often as a vain woman changes her apparel) there resided a ruined ivory castle, nearly grown over with nettles, next to a great rushing river that appeared to flow backward—going up waterfalls instead of down. Sprawled beside the island's main harbor was a ramshackle pirate village, easily identified, even from Jocelyn's lofty height, by the smell of blood and rum. And in the distance she spied a graceful flight of dragons performing an aerial ballet, their scales shimmering in the morning sun. Though she couldn't tell for certain from her vantage point, Jocelyn did not expect to find a single corset on the entire island. She was utterly charmed.

Even so, the girl knew that somewhere down there, amidst all the wonder, a terrible beast was waiting.

Reminds me a bit of my first wedding day.

Edgar deposited Jocelyn on the harbor dock at the edge of the pirate village. Before he flew away, she handed him the apology letter she had written. "Could you please

find a way to deliver this to my friend, Roger? He used to live at the school, though I'm not sure where he is now."

The courier agreed to try to find the boy—free of charge, in honor of Jocelyn's late father. He did not display even the slightest hint of annoyance at having to fly all the way back to the mainland to find someone with no address and deliver a letter that might have easily been dropped off the night before.

That Edgar, he was a professional.

With a little hop and a flap of his wings, the great bird took flight. Jocelyn watched as he soared high into the sky, a tiny sting of jealousy pricking at her heart. If only she could break the bonds holding her to the earth. If only she could be that free.

Long before Edgar disappeared in the distance, she brought her eyes back to the horizon and surveyed her surroundings. Rough wooden planks, barnacled and weathered gray from spray and salt, formed a tangled web of docking that stretched as far down the beach as Jocelyn could see. A miasma of overripe fish, gun smoke, and unwashed bodies hung in the briny air. Schooners, sloops, frigates, cutters, and many other varieties of ships in various conditions were moored offshore. Sailors swarmed over their surfaces like roaches on leftovers, inspecting rigging and performing repairs. Before her eyes, a brawl broke out on the deck of a twenty-gunner. The air was filled with sounds of the roaring sea, screaming gulls, shouted curses, breaking glass, and breaking bones.

A wide smile grew on the girl's face. For the first time in her life, Jocelyn felt truly at home.

Now to find this Mr. Smee.

As she looked about for someone to ask for directions, a man approached her. In manner and appearance he presented himself a bit more finely than the men Jocelyn had observed on the ships. She took an instant dislike to him.

"You there, girl, have you only just arrived from the mainland?"

A hint of culture and education rounded the corners of the man's voice. Jocelyn made her own voice extra pointy to compensate. "And what business is that of yours?"

"Why, the business of harbormaster, of course. It is my duty to monitor all comings and goings. Keep out the riffraff, the bankers, the missionaries, and other such unsavories. So I ask again: have you just arrived?"

Jocelyn would have preferred to ignore the man, but she did need directions. "Yes, I flew in with a courier crow. Can you tell me—"

"I'll do the inquiring around here, thank you. Once I am finished, you may ask a question of me." He pulled a ledger from his satchel. Then he licked the end of a lead pencil, cleared his throat, and said, "Must keep the paperwork in order. Now then: When, pray tell, are you from?"

"*When?* Don't you mean *where?*"

The harbormaster snapped his book closed and fixed the girl with what he likely thought of as his most penetrating stare. "I most certainly do not mean *where*. I already know that you are not from one of the Neverland's many indigenous tribes; ergo, you must be from the mainland. If you are not from *here*, you are from *there*. Any fool can deduce that."

Jocelyn crossed her arms and scowled. "How can you possibly want to know when I came from? Isn't it obvious? I came from today. Yesterday, if you want to be more specific."

The harbormaster sighed loudly. "No. No. No. I'm asking, roughly, what year you are from. If you don't know exactly, you can give me your best guess."

Jocelyn looked up and down the dock. Surely someone else could tell her how to find Mr. Smee. Unfortunately, no one else appeared. She returned the harbormaster's sigh and answered, "I turned thirteen yesterday."

"I don't care to know your age, child. Allow me to simplify matters for you. When you woke up this morning in your pretty little bed, who was king? Was it Sweyn Forkbeard? William the Conqueror? Richard the Lionheart? Henry the Eightieth?"

This was getting ridiculous. "I didn't wake up in a bed this morning. I've been traveling all night, and your questions are the stupidest ones I've ever heard. Henry the Eightieth? There is no such person. Everyone knows that King George sits upon the throne."

If Jocelyn, who was rather a sharp girl, was a bit flummoxed by this line of questioning, I imagine you may be even more confused. I'll speak slowly to help you understand. Children who visit the Neverland come from as many *Whens* as *Wheres*. The Neverland is clever that way.

"King George," he spoke aloud as he noted her reply. "Next, what is the purpose of your visit? Plunder? Murder? Revenge?"

Jocelyn glared at the man. "Principally revenge, though I am keeping my options open."

"Have you anything to declare?"

"Yes. I declare these asinine questions to be a waste of my time."

The harbormaster made another mark in his ledger. "Noted. One last question, though I should have started with it, I suppose. Name, please."

"Jocelyn Hook."

The harbormaster snapped his pencil lead on his paper, making a nasty black mark. "Hook, eh?" The smooth corners of his voice now shook around the edges. "Why didn't you say so? Welcome to the Neverland, my dear. I suppose you've come to settle your father's affairs?"

Jocelyn was finished with the man's questions. "Where can I find a Mr. Smee?"

"Mr. Smee, of course! I'd be happy to give you

directions and anything else you may require. Only...
be wary. Smee has not been, shall we say, 'quite right,'
since your father's untimely passing."

The harbormaster gave Jocelyn directions to a tailor
shop a few blocks inland, and Jocelyn happily turned her
back to him. As she strolled away, he called out, "Good
luck, young miss!" The sound of fluttering ledger pages
followed the girl up the dock.

The pirate village sprawled over the land. Haphazard
buildings, shoddily constructed from driftwood and
old ship parts, tilted drunkenly over its cobbled street.
Garishly painted ladies (with, as Jocelyn had suspected,
nary a corset in sight) leaned out windows, exchanging
insults with passersby below. Packs of men, scoundrels
and blaggards, each one of them, lazed about, swapping
rum and tales on stoops and street corners. Everyone
Jocelyn spied, man or woman, was armed to the teeth
with cutlasses and pistols, daggers and bombs. The girl
regretted her lack of a weapon. For the first time in her
life, Jocelyn felt the hot shame of being underdressed
for a party.

I expect you are wondering why the pirate village was
so bustling. You are likely operating under the mistaken
assumption that Captain Hook and the crew of the *Jolly
Roger* were the only pirates ever to sail the Neverland's
seas. That had been true at one time—when the captain

was in a predigested state—as his fierce reputation kept other pirates from infringing upon his territory. However, after Hook's death, scads of new pirates moved in to fill the void, creating a land rush around Hangman's Harbor. The building boom brought all kinds of rogues and rascals to the village. In addition to an influx of sailors and shipbuilders, a whole horde of villains immigrated: saloon keepers, rumrunners, even a mortgage banker or two, all hoping to cash in.

Jocelyn turned down a side street, passing a market stand filled with fresh fish and blasting caps. She recognized a broken rudder, now pressed into service as signage above a tailor shop. If she could find the crocodile as easily as she seemed to have found Mr. Smee, Jocelyn might have her revenge buttoned up by teatime. She entered the shop, ready to confront her destiny.

CHAPTER FOURTEEN

*Wherein Jocelyn Acquires
a Dangerous New Pet*

Upon meeting Mr. Smee, many a foolish
young girl has expressed the bizarre wish to
keep him as a pet pirate. Even Jocelyn was
not entirely inclined to disagree with that idiotic senti-
ment, though she felt that housebreaking might prove
to be difficult.

Picture a weathered and fierce Santa Claus in mis-
matched stockings, with a deadly sharp cutlass strapped
to his waist. Add a sunny, yet mildly threatening, dispo-
sition that everyone seems to enjoy—even those unfortunate enough to be killed by Smee generally die thinking,
What a dear little man.

If your imagination is half as good as my storytelling (not likely), you'll have a fairly good sense of the old

pirate Jocelyn found mending a threadbare doublet inside the tailor's shop.

Smee kept up a conversation as he worked. "Look at these fine stitches. That's the way, ain't it, Johnny? We've seen and repaired far worse holes than this when we were sailing with the captain, rest his soul. Why, he'd have torn all his fancy clothes to shreds with that hook of his if we weren't there to help him get dressed in the morning."

Jocelyn cleared her throat to get his attention. Smee peered over his spectacles with a rather pleasant scowl. "Well now, Johnny, it seems to me that we have some company. Get along now, miss; my shop is no place for children. I've got needles and other sharp things lying about. A little girl, such as yourself, might get hurt."

Little girl?

Jocelyn pulled herself up to her full height and glared at the man. "Never you mind about needles. I've had enough of them to last a lifetime. You are Mr. Smee, I presume? I am Jocelyn Hook, daughter of Captain Jam—"

Smee jumped to his feet, interrupting Jocelyn and scattering several spools of thread in his excitement. "My dear Captain Hook! Yes, yes, of course. Well, Jocelyn Hook, as I live and breathe. You look just like your mother. Except for the parts that look like your father. And the parts that look like no one I've ever seen. Where do you think those parts come from, Johnny? Ah, never mind. We don't want to pry now, do we?" Beaming, he grabbed her hand and forcefully shook it up and down.

"You knew my mother?" The borders surrounding the empty place in Jocelyn's heart gave a little twinge. She glared at the man in retaliation.

Smee ignored her dark expression and clapped his free hand over his mouth (his other still pumping the girl's arm as though the well had gone dry). "Whaaa nobbb apaaaassed aa taaaak aaaabt eeeer."

Jocelyn yanked out of his grasp and rubbed her shoulder. "I'll thank you to keep your hands to yourself. Better yet, keep them in your pockets. I can't understand a word you are saying."

Smee put both hands in his pockets, looked around the shop, and whispered, "We're not supposed to speak about your mum. And anyway," he went on in a normal tone of voice, "we've got other things to talk over now, don't we? Look at you—Jocelyn Hook! Here in our shop at last. We're just so pleased to be making your acquaintanceship! I was a great friend of your father's, I was. A bit of a mentor to him, really. Things haven't been the same for us since he was, begging your pardon, eaten. Isn't that right, Johnny?"

Jocelyn looked around the small shop. It was cluttered with bobbins, pattern pieces, and articles of clothing in need of repair, but as far as she could tell, no one else was present. "Who is Johnny?"

"Oh, bless my soul! Please forgive me, young Miss Hook. This here's Johnny Corkscrew." Smee unsheathed his sword and held it up to Jocelyn for inspection. She peered at the blade with a mixture of confusion and amusement. "Next to the captain he's the best friend and most trustworthy companion I ever had."

This might have been what the harbormaster had been talking about when he'd said Smee was not "quite right." A hint of a smile formed on Jocelyn's lips. "I see. Johnny is your sword?"

Smee yanked his weapon back, stuffing it into its sheath. "Johnny is no mere sword. Don't insult him." He patted the hilt lovingly. "He's a cutlass, made of the finest Damascus steel. He's got a smelted copper grip and . . ." He trailed off and stared hard at Jocelyn. "You're not here about mending, are you?"

"Mending?"

"You know . . ." Smee pantomimed threading a needle and sewing something.

Jocelyn shook her head and pulled her father's letter from her dress pocket. Smee took one look at it and burst into sloppy, wet tears.

"The letter!" he sobbed. "We know all about that, don't we, J-J-Johnny? The captain, he wrote it up and gave it to our keeping. He was having night visions, you know? Terrors of the beast. He seemed to know what was going to happen. 'Smee!' he'd say to me. 'Smee! With Davy

Jones as my witness, I will not be defeated by that inso-
lent boy, yet I know in my bones that the ticking beast
will be my doom.' He g-g-gave us the letter and told us to
get it to his little daughter on the mainland after the..."
He swallowed. "After the deed was done."

Jocelyn awkwardly patted the man's arm. "There,
there. Don't cry. Please. Just don't."

Smee took a large handkerchief from his back pocket
and began mopping up his face. "The captain, he told
us to use that great black bird. So we did, and I guess
the bird did, and now you did, er...done..." He took
a shuddering breath. "What I mean to say is: now that
you're here and all, are you hungry?" He didn't wait for
a reply before he began clearing stacks of clothing from
his worktable.

Jocelyn's stomach rumbled, but the man's mood swings
appeared to be as violent as his handshake. "I really don't
want to trouble you—"

"Trouble me! Trouble me? Well now, Johnny, what
do you think of that? The girl doesn't want to trouble
me!" Mr. Smee opened a cupboard and pulled out a mis-
matched set of dishes. "Did anyone ever wonder if it was
troublesome to row a leaky dinghy fourteen furlongs in
blinding rain to return to land and get the captain's favorite smoking jacket? How about spending a hot afternoon
in the galley trying to bake a light and fluffy cake filled
with poison so vile it'd break my skin out in boils from

only the vapors coming off it? Was that any trouble for Mr. Smee? Or having to fight off hundreds of bees as long as my little finger, and me being allergic and all, just to get honey for the captain's afternoon tea! Was that any trouble?" Smee punctuated his speech with slams and crashes as he violently set the table, which was shoved into a corner, barely visible behind stacked bolts of cloth, piles of clothing, and the flotsam and jetsam one might expect in a tailor shop.

"Well..." Jocelyn tried to figure out what the right answer might be. "No?"

Smee banged down a butter dish. "Of course not! And getting you a bit of grub won't be either. Make no mistake about that!"

That sealed it. Jocelyn was entirely won over by the old pirate. She seated herself at the head of the table, where she enjoyed a cheery meal of tea, burned toast, and tinned sardines. Smee even offered Jocelyn a bit of stale cake, but remembering the aforementioned poison, she declined.

After their meal, Mr. Smee led Jocelyn up to a dusty attic room. Tucked away in the corner lay an old wooden trunk covered in ornate carvings. From a leather string tied round his neck, he produced a weighty brass key, then bowed and left Jocelyn alone.

The trunk's rusty hinges complained as Jocelyn lifted its heavy lid. An elegant red jacket trimmed in gold braid lay folded neatly on the top of its contents. The girl brought it to her nose and breathed in a faint scent of cigar smoke and salty air. She stood and put it on. The jacket was far too big, nearly dragging on the floor, but it was warm and comforting. Jocelyn rolled up the sleeves and returned to the trunk's cargo, examining each artifact before carefully laying it on the floor in front of her.

It felt strange to be surrounded by things her father had touched—things that he had specifically set aside for her. She imagined that some of the items would be quite useful in her upcoming adventure: a heavy brass spyglass, a gleaming silver sword, and a (rather small) bag filled with pieces of eight.

Others were strange, or at least strange things to leave a young girl, like the half-dozen cans of Mrs. Flint's Hook Polish and Mustache Wax or the silver cigar holder made to hold two cigars at once. There was also a small iron box, engraved on top with the image of a hook. Jocelyn tried to open it, but it was locked tight, with no key in sight. She resolved to ask Smee about it later. Perhaps he had that key as well.

When at last the trunk was empty, Jocelyn surveyed the things around her and was struck again by how little she knew about her father. It hit her with a new clarity: The great Captain Hook was dead. They would never have the great adventure she had dreamed of. Jocelyn was on her own.

Her fingers sought his letter, tucked away in her

pocket, but she did not pull it out to read again. There was no need—she knew nearly every word by heart. Her father had called this quest her inheritance. She would spend it well.

"Mr. Smee," Jocelyn called down the stairs, "let the adventure begin!"

CHAPTER FIFTEEN

The Neverland's Finest

You must forgive me at this point for skipping ahead in the narrative.

Or don't. I don't care much either way.

The next few days were busy but dull. The girl may have called for the adventure to begin, but in my opinion that was merely dramatic foolishness.

Jocelyn spent her time in the pirate village arranging for the delivery and loading of goods while Mr. Smee used the greater part of her inherited gold in order to procure a small, single-masted sloop. He insisted on spending a bit more to have the captain's quarters redecorated, so as to be more fitting for a young Captain Hook. Jocelyn didn't much care, as long as her cabin wasn't pink.

With the ship secured and ready, Jocelyn appointed

Smee bo'sun and tasked him with hiring the fiercest, bravest, and most experienced group of pirates in the village as crew.

Hiring a pirate crew sounds exciting, doesn't it?

It wasn't.

Smee's hours were spent asking questions such as: "Tell me—and Johnny—about your last job. What were your reasons for leaving? What is your educational background? Has a disagreement with an employer ever led to dismemberment or disemboweling?"

See what I mean? Dull. Skipping ahead.

Jocelyn stood proud at the bow of her very own ship, still wrapped in the too-large embrace of her father's red jacket. There was a gentle sea breeze blowing one unruly lock of hair about her face. If she had been able to see herself, the girl would have been surprised to notice she looked very much like the portrait of her father hanging round her neck. Jocelyn had an unmistakable tang of captainship about her.

It had only been a few days since her departure from finishing school, but she already felt as if her life there had been nothing other than a bad dream.

Except . . . she did miss Roger.

Jocelyn wondered if Edgar had been able to deliver her letter, and if so, had it been read?

Her fingers traced the cool metal of Roger's compass,

buried deep in her pocket, and she wished, not for the first time, that he had been able to come along. They were supposed to have an adventure together. That had been Roger's promise, but Jocelyn felt as if she had broken it.

The girl forced her mind away from those thoughts and back toward the present. For as long as she could remember, Jocelyn had dreamed of captaining her own ship. As soon as Mr. Smee returned with the finest crew the Neverland had to offer, she would set sail, having nearly everything she ever wanted.

As if he had been summoned by her thoughts, Mr. Smee appeared. "Begging your pardon, miss, but I've done it. Your men will be arriving soon."

Jocelyn was thrilled. "My own crew, at last! Quick, tell me, Smee, are they everything I had hoped for? Brave? Fierce as bloodthirsty dogs? Men my father would have been proud to call his own?"

Smee gazed out to sea, as though searching for something. "Well, er, that is to say…"

"All right, perhaps my father would not have been exactly *proud*; I'm sure he was a hard man to please. They are brave, though?"

"Brave? I wouldn't exactly—"

Jocelyn interrupted. "Are they fierce and bloodthirsty?"

"Thirsty? To be sure. But, fierce? Well…that's a mite strong—"

"I can scarcely believe it, Smee: Captain Jocelyn Hook

is about to set sail with her own ferocious band of pirates. That crocodile doesn't stand a chance. I'd wager a guess that even Blackbeard's men at their best couldn't hold a candle to the Neverland's finest. Right, Smee?"

Smee continued staring at the horizon. He looked a bit ill.

"Smee?" Jocelyn's triumphant smile withered. "Tell me—you have hired the best crew that could be found in the village, haven't you?"

He dropped his eyes to Johnny Corkscrew in an appeal for help. None came. He cleared his throat and mumbled, "No, miss."

"Oh. I would have liked the best, but . . . second best, perhaps?"

"Not exactly."

Jocelyn began to worry. "Third? Fourth?"

Mr. Smee squirmed under her questioning. "No, miss."

"Out with it, Smee!" she roared, sounding quite a lot like the prior Captain Hook. "What kind of crew did you hire for me?"

"Ah, well, strictly speaking, miss, as a matter of rank, your crew comes in squarely at *sixteenth* best in the Neverland."

It was unfortunate news for Jocelyn that the Neverland hosted only sixteen available crews at the time. Every last one of them had turned up for the interview process, eager to sail under Hook's flag and assist his heir in such an illustrious quest. However, each had promptly turned down the job upon learning that said heir was barely more than a child, and a girl to boot. Smee had only just managed to hire the last, and worst, crew that he interviewed: a motley assortment of characters desperate to make a name for themselves.

Jocelyn stood at the top of the gangplank as her men boarded the ship. Smee was on hand to make introductions and provide commentary. The first to arrive was One-Armed Jack.

The girl wondered at his unusual name. Unless her eyes were deceiving her, he had two good arms (though under her gaze he quickly tucked one inside his shirt), yet here he was introducing himself and saying, "Happy to meet you, Cap'n. I'd offer to shake your hand, but as I've only got the one, and it being full o' me gear..."

Jocelyn thought to question his strange behavior, but she noticed Smee shaking his head. Instead she said, "Welcome aboard, Jack. You may stow your things below deck."

As One-Armed Jack walked away, carrying his trunk in one hand and scratching his hindquarters with the other, Jocelyn turned to Smee and demanded, "What was that about?"

He ducked his head and replied, "Begging your pardon, miss, but your men have some...how shall we put this, Johnny? Some unusual characteristics. You see, they've not had much experience. Not like your regular crews. None of them have even been in a real battle, but that doesn't stop them from wishing they had, so they, ah, pretend."

"That's ridiculous. Anyone with eyes could see that that man has two arms. How can he get away with pretending he doesn't?"

Mr. Smee looked away, watching another pirate limp his way up the gangplank. "Ridiculous, yes, well, it might be a mite ridiculous—yet they all go along with it. You see, if, say, Jim McCraig with a Wooden Leg here," he motioned to the man boarding the ship, "was to point out that Jack had two arms, then Jack could say that Jim doesn't really have a wooden leg; he's only got a corroded old sliver in his big toe. See there, that's what causes the limp. So aye, it may be silly, but, begging your pardon, it works, see."

At this point Jim McCraig with a Wooden Leg reached the deck. When he addressed his new captain, though, Jocelyn was hard-pressed to decipher much of what he said. His words appeared to be a delinquent cousin of English—faintly familiar, but mostly jumble and noise. She leaned over to Smee and whispered, "Is he pretending to have something wrong with his tongue as well?"

Smee whispered back, "No. In this case something really *is* wrong with his tongue: he's Scottish. I believe he just introduced himself."

Jocelyn turned back to Jim, considering. "Mr. McCraig, I see that you are missing one of your limbs. I hope its absence will not cause you to be lax in your duties, for I plan to run a tight ship and have no room for those who are unable to pull their own weight. You will be required to do as much as a sailor with two good legs."

The man replied with another enthusiastic string of gibberish. Smee translated: "He says it won't hold him back. Matter of fact, might be dead useful at times. Jim can tell when a storm is brewing by the phantom itch where his meat leg used to be."

"Very good, Jim. Be sure and let me know if that happens."

The crew was rounded out by the arrival of Nubbins, the cook, and Blind Bart, the ship's lookout. Nubbins was the only crew member with a real battle wound. Smee explained that the man had lost his left thumb in an unfortunate cooking accident, but claimed that it had been bitten off by a giant squid. Nubbins liked to brag that he'd gotten his revenge by transforming the creature into a delicious dish of calamari with capers—served cold, of course.

Blind Bart seemed an unusual choice for lookout, as he wore patches over both eyes. His reasoning here was elegantly simple: if one eye patch made a pirate look fierce and dangerous, two would make him look doubly so. (The man also had a fear of drowning—an unfortunate quality in a sailor—but as even the stupidest toddler knows, covering your eyes makes you invisible. Thus, if the ocean couldn't see him, it couldn't get him.) Though her pirates were certainly odd, Jocelyn was in no position to turn even a single one away. She was running with a skeleton crew as it was. Her ship would need every man to do his part.

The young captain called her men together before they left the harbor. "Let the dreadful crocodile beware, for I now christen this ship the *Hook's Revenge*. Hoist anchor, find the eye of the wind, and let's be under way!"

The crew cheered. Mr. Smee cried. One-Armed Jack clumsily raised a black flag emblazoned with the image of a large red hook. The ship's sails filled with wind, and she proudly set out to sea.

CHAPTER SIXTEEN

High-Sea High Jinks

AS soon as the *Hook's Revenge* reached open waters, Jocelyn ordered her crew to gather on the main deck. "All right, you dogs, we are on an important and dangerous mission. As you know, my father, Captain James Hook…"

All the men shuddered.

"…is dead, viciously slain at the jaws of the Neverland's crocodile. It is my duty—nay, my privilege—to avenge him. Who is with me?"

The crew whooped and hollered "Aye, aye, Captain!" (With the exception of Smee, who was still happily sobbing into his handkerchief.) Jocelyn felt heartened by their enthusiasm. With such spirit on her side, defeating the crocodile should be easy. She imagined how it might play out:

Jocelyn's men would be gathered behind her, cheering. She would stroll up to the beast and tap it on the shoulder. . . . Do crocodiles have shoulders? They must; they have arms, don't they? Or are they all legs?

She tried to remember what, if anything, she had read about crocodile anatomy. Nothing helpful came to mind. Making a mental note to look through her books, Jocelyn continued with her fantasy.

Shoulders or not, she'd tap it somewhere, and say, "Excuse me. You may remember eating my father, Captain Hook? I'm here to avenge his death. Farewell, hideous beast." Then she would poke the creature with her sword and it would die. With its dying breath, it would say:

"CANNONBALL!"

Cannonball?

Jocelyn drew her attention back to the deck. It was in a state of utter pandemonium. A line of men had formed at the plank. They were using it as a diving board, hence the "cannonball" that had interrupted her daydream. A dripping-wet One-Armed Jack, apparently forgetting his missing arm, climbed up the anchor chain. Near the middle of the deck, as far as possible from the water, Blind Bart was trying to start a game of Marco Polo.

Smee was still crying.

The air was filled with shouts of *me hearty*, *arr*, and *bucko* as the men all tried to outpirate each other. Jocelyn needed to gain control before the crew tore her ship apart. She clapped her hands. She whistled. She stomped her foot. Nothing happened; the crew hardly noticed her.

"Attention on deck! The next to speak out of turn will...will walk the plank!" That did no good. With the exception of Bart, they all wanted to walk the plank.

"Settle down or I'll keelhaul you!"

The only response she received from that was a chorus of "Me first!"

Jocelyn wondered what her father would think of her crew and felt ashamed. She climbed to the poop deck so as to tower over the foolish men below her. "Listen up, you miserable powder monkeys!" she roared. "Shut up and be still, or face my wrath!" The girl truly had no idea what her wrath might be, but neither did her crew. The men gave her their attention.

"We're sorry, Mother," she heard one of them say.

"Mother? Mother! Which of you dogs dares to call me *mother*?" She didn't wait for a reply. "I am not your mother. I am your captain, and you would be wise to address me as such. We have no need for a mother on this ship. I have lived my entire life without one, and I never missed a thing. Are we clear on the matter?"

The crew nodded, wide-eyed, at their fierce captain.

"Men," Jocelyn went on in a slightly calmer tone,

"while your enthusiasm is not wholly unappreciated, your behavior is not befitting your station. This is no pleasure cruise! We must find and kill the Neverland's crocodile. Any more of this foolishness and I will cast anchor in ye!"

Smee applauded wildly, looking fit to burst with pride. The rest of the men reluctantly joined in.

Jocelyn continued her speech. "The crocodile is dangerous. It is wily. We will need all our wits about us. We will need courage. We will need . . ." She stopped to consider what else would be necessary. "We will need to find it. Does anyone know where the beast lives? Mr. Smee?"

"No, Miss Captain, I'm afraid I don't. We used to know it was around by the ticking clock in its belly—at least until the end." He took off his spectacles and wiped his eyes. "The croc's clock stopped ticking for a time, you know. That's how the beast was able to . . . to do what it did to the poor captain. But it started ticking again soon after. Maybe we'll hear it somewhere."

Nubbins timidly raised his hand. "Cap'n Jo? I'm not sure of the truth of this, but someone from my dinner club—er, I mean my drinking, cussing, and carousing club—*arr!*"

The other men shouted *"Arr!"* in reply.

Jocelyn glared at them until they looked away, ashamed.

Nubbins went on, addressing his feet. "This fellow from my club went out to Salmagundi Island to gather cuttings of wild lavender, uh, to brew into a sort of, um, flower whiskey—potent stuff, it is. So he went out to gather the lavender and as he rowed away, he heard a ticking sound coming from one of the island's sea caves. Scared him something terrible; thought it was a bomb, he did. Might not a been, though, right? It could be the croc's on that island."

The increase of pirates in the area since Captain Hook's death had led to a need for more places to bury treasure and maroon people. To fill that need, the Neverland had broken off some pieces of itself and sent them out into the sea to form a smaller chain of islands. Salmagundi was the largest and most popular in the chain.

Blind Bart spoke up. "If there is a clock to be heard anywhere on, around, above, or below there, I will hear it." (As he was unable to rely on his sense of sight, Bart made up for it with extraordinary hearing.)

No one had any better ideas on where to find the beast so Jocelyn set their heading for the long voyage to Salmagundi Island in order to look—or *listen*, as it were—for the crocodile.

"Tonight we feast!" Jocelyn called to her men.

Nubbins looked over the galley stores and whipped up a delightful meal: tarragon-scented salt pork with sauerkraut and hardtack topped with lime-ginger crème. One-Armed Jack passed out beverages, managing quite well with his one arm by switching to the other whenever he tired.

Jim McCraig sang, surprising Jocelyn and the rest of the crew with the clarity of his words. In song, strangely enough, his bizarre accent became quite easy to understand:

Yo ho ho and a bottle o' rum,
My mum thinks I am jist a bum,
She hoped I'd become a social worker
But I'm a sailin' mad berserker....
I'll ne'er go home again! Yo ho!
She can't make me go home again!

It was the best party Jocelyn had ever attended. She ate with her fingers and threw her scraps to the floor. She danced on the table, soaking her skirts with grog and gravy. She sang along with her men, her sweet voice matching theirs in enthusiasm (and surpassing them in pitch), and found herself heartily agreeing—she never wanted to go home again either. The pirate life was even better than she had dreamed.

CHAPTER SEVENTEEN

In Which a Daring Rescue
Does Not Occur

It would take Captain Jocelyn and her crew a few days to reach their destination. The men spent their time listening to Smee tell...not exactly lies, but perhaps a few exaggerations, about his escapades with Captain Hook. As to be expected, the bo'sun was a bit of a hero among the young pirates—a fact that did not bother him in the least. While the men talked, Jocelyn took up her inherited sword and sparred with her shadow on the main deck. Even if killing the crocodile turned out to be as easy as she'd imagined, it wouldn't hurt to practice.

You may be surprised at her confidence. I have found that it is easy to be self-assured when you are untested—particularly if you are well-read. Once you get out in the world, away from the library, you may find that things are not quite as clear as they seemed when you held the whole universe between leather covers. For example, I once read a book about getting rid of unwanted pests. I felt that I was quite the expert, and yet here you sit.

Now, let's see, Jocelyn thought. *Was it shuffle-shuffle, thrust? Or thrust, shuffle-shuffle?*

A dark speck in the sky caught her attention, interrupting her musings. For a moment she thought it might be Edgar, perhaps bringing a message from Roger, but those hopes quickly fizzled. Closer inspection revealed a person, a boy to be exact, attired in clothes made from skeleton leaves and tree sap. Jocelyn recognized him as the boy she had dreamed about on her first night at finishing school. He did a series of barrel rolls and a few loop-de-loops before alighting on the ship's railing with a rather self-satisfied look on his face. Jocelyn found him far less impressive than he found himself.

"Hello, girl," the boy said. "I don't remember bringing you here. How did you end up on a pirate ship?" He pulled a dagger from his belt, looked around, and gnashed his teeth. "No need to tell me now. I'm sure you are terribly frightened. Don't worry; I'll rescue you."

Jocelyn turned her back on him, stuck her nose in the

air, and said, "I do not need rescuing, and *you* did not bring me here, thank you very much!" She sheathed her sword and brushed at imaginary lint on the sleeve of her father's jacket.

The boy flew off the rail and sat cross-legged on the deck in front of her. "You're welcome," he replied. "If you want to stay here, that's all right with me. You go ahead and start telling the story while I keep an eye on the pirates."

"What on earth are you talking about?"

He rolled his eyes and spoke slowly. "Stories. Like the lady that pricks her finger and eats an apple before she has to take a nap. Or the lady that can't sleep because she has pee in her bed."

"It is not *pee*; it is *a pea*. And I am not here to tell you stories!" She turned her back on him again.

"Aren't you here to be a mother to me and the lost boys? Mothers tell stories, and they do the washing, and the mending, and the scolding. Although if you want to forget about the scolding, I won't mind. But mothers must tell stories." He stretched out his legs and kicked his heels on the deck. "If you don't tell me a story right now, I shan't take my medicine tonight and you will be sorry!"

Jocelyn whirled back to face him. "I am most certainly not here to be your mother. What is the obsession with mothers here? You and those lost boys will just have to wash, mend, and story yourselves. I have my own business to attend to. Now go away." She punctuated that last bit with a stomp of her foot.

The boy laughed and said, "Fine, fine, you don't want to be our mother—even though you're really good at the scolding part. I'll still rescue you." He stood and grabbed her by the arm.

Jocelyn slapped his hand away. "For the last time, I don't need rescuing!"

"If you don't need rescuing, what are you doing on a pirate ship? This is no place for a girl."

It seemed there would never be a shortage of people willing to doubt Jocelyn's abilities. "What business could I have on a pirate ship? The business of captain! I am Captain Jocelyn Hook, and this is my ship, the *Hook's Revenge!*"

The boy crowed with joy and said, "Well, Girl Captain, I'm glad you are here. I do love a good war." He arranged his face into a fierce scowl, leaped to his feet, and pointed his dagger at her. "If you are here for revenge against me, you will be disappointed. You will die as your father before you!"

Revenge against him? *This strange, arrogant boy?*

Comparing him to the beast her father had described was like comparing a flea to a king cobra. Certainly they could both bite, but only one was deadly. "I am not here to fight you, silly boy!" she laughed at him. "I'm here to have my revenge on the crocodile. When I am done with that, if you'd still like to have a war, perhaps I'll oblige you. That is, if I'm not too busy." Deciding that she had had enough of him, Jocelyn turned away and resumed practicing her swordplay. Her shadow stuck out its tongue at the boy before taking up its sword and joining in.

According to my sources on the Neverland, that was the first time that Peter Pan could find nothing clever to say. He glared at Jocelyn and boasted, "I have a fairy!" Then, with the air of one who has put another in their rightful place, he thumbed his nose and flew away.

Jocelyn was still trying to puzzle out the strange encounter when Blind Bart called out, "Land ho! I can hear waves breaking on her rocky shore, and the air is perfumed with wild lavender. It can only be Salmagundi Island! We will reach her just as the evening crickets begin to chirp—or for those of you who depend on your eyes, at twilight." He was rather verbose for a lookout. "I think . . . no, I am certain—I hear a faint ticking!"

Guided by both Blind Bart's keen sense of hearing and Smee's piloting knowledge, Jocelyn steered the ship into an inlet dotted with caves. Bart claimed the ticking was coming from the third one on the left.

The young captain, beginning to feel a little anxious, ordered that one of the dinghies be let down immediately.

In shipman's terms, a dinghy is a small boat kept aboard a larger vessel—useful for stealthy landings, navigating shallow beaches, and giving people an excuse to say "dinghy" without their mothers becoming cross. Most ships have one, but Blind Bart had firmly requested that the *Hook's Revenge* carry three: the main, a spare, and a spare-spare, for safety reasons. His petition for a spare-spare-spare had been denied, as it would have left no room for the cannon.

Jocelyn chose Smee and One-Armed Jack to accompany her. Before climbing in, she commanded her men. "Bart, keep a weather ear out for that crocodile. If you hear ticking leave the cave, sound the alarm. In that case, Jim, Nubbins—one of you must fire the cannon to alert me. Should I hear its blast, I'll know the beast is on the move."

Having issued all the commands, there was nothing left for the girl to do but climb into the little boat and complete her father's legacy.

My, but that sounds dramatic, doesn't it?

CHAPTER EIGHTEEN

Jack Is Disarmed

If you have ever felt a bit nervous about a task before you—such as walking past a snarling dog on your way to school, confessing to your mother that you broke her favorite Royal Family commemorative plate, or needing to dig up and rebury a body on a cold, dark night—you may have an idea of how Jocelyn felt as she seated herself in the little boat.

Her hands shook as she reached for the oars, but Smee beat her to them. "We can't let you row, miss. Can we, Johnny?" he said, jostling her out of position.

Noting that Smee spoke more often to Johnny when he was nervous or unsettled did little to restore Jocelyn's confidence. "And why not?" she snapped. "Because I'm a

girl? I am becoming very tired of people thinking I can't do things!"

"No, miss. Not because you're a girl. That doesn't have a thing to do with it. Johnny Corkscrew and me are going to row because you're the captain and rowing is work best suited for men of lesser worth. *Your* job is to sit back and yell at us to go faster."

He pulled Johnny from his sheath and motioned with it to a suddenly nervous One-Armed Jack. "And this one here can't row unless you want to go in circles. His job is to hold an umbrella over your head to keep you from getting splashed. That's how we did it with the first Captain Hook, may the devil take his dear soul, and that's how we're going to do it with you, miss. Right, Johnny?" Johnny must have agreed, for Smee beamed at the blade and lovingly resheathed it, much to One-Armed Jack's apparent relief.

Jocelyn did want to do things the way her father would have. By way of an apology to Smee, she took her seat and yelled, "Well, what are we waiting for, scum? Get rowing!"

"That's just the way your father would have done it." Smee pulled out his handkerchief and wiped his eyes before grabbing the oars. "If you ever want to give me a hard kick to my backside, I'd be obliged to you. It'd be just like the old days!"

By this time the sun had sunk halfway below the

horizon. The sky was streaked with pink and orange clouds. The evening was warm and comfortable. A sweet scent of wild lavender wafted from the island, mixing with the briny sea air. Jocelyn might have been on a pleasure cruise, had it not been for the ominous task at hand—rather, the ominous task at hand *and* the two sweaty pirates in the boat with her. They were difficult to ignore.

Jack held the umbrella, but it did little to keep the spray off, for in his excitement he neglected to open it. He waved it about, yelling "Arrr!" every few minutes.

Smee was a bit more practiced at his role. His pulls on the oars were strong and smooth. And the more Jocelyn abused him, the faster he rowed.

They approached the cave. In the shadow of evening, it was as ominous as a great gaping maw, waiting to tear them into pieces and swallow the bits. However, it was not the mouth of the *cave* that would soon clamp over tender flesh, severing muscle and bone . . . but I am getting ahead of myself.

As Smee steered the dinghy into the cavern's yawning opening, Jocelyn looked back the way they came. The *Hook's Revenge* made a black silhouette against the darkening sea. Fire-breathing dragonflies darted over the gray waves, taunting foolish fish beneath. An acrid smell of burned cod hung in the air. One lonely star blinked in the sky. For the briefest of moments, the girl considered a wish, but thought better of it. Jocelyn would take her chances and defeat the crocodile on her own.

She turned to face the darkness.

"Jack, put down that umbrella and light a lantern."

The lamp created a thin circle of light around their boat, barely holding back the gloom. Over the soft creak and splash of the oars, they heard it, faint but distinct: ticking.

One-Armed Jack held the lantern out. Near the cave opening, reflected in the lamplight, ripples formed in the sea—first small, then larger. Jocelyn leaned over the edge of the boat for a closer look. Her jacket hem trailed in the water.

The ticking grew louder.

"Steady, boys, here it comes," the girl whispered with forced courage. She rolled up her sleeves. Grasping her sword in one hand and her locket in the other, she waited. A few boat lengths away, the crocodile surfaced.

"Captain," Smee whispered, "it's gotten bigger since I saw it last."

Its head alone must have been nearly half the length of the dinghy. Fear squeezed its way into the small boat, jostling the passengers and taking up far more than its fair share of room.

One-Armed Jack shrank back, pulling the lantern toward him. Shadows closed in. He mumbled a prayer under his breath.

The beast approached. The now loud ticktock of the creature's internal clock filled the cave. Jocelyn braced herself, ready to strike. She intended to shout, but her voice came out barely louder than a whisper. "In the name of my father, Captain James Hook, prepare to meet your doom."

The crocodile whipped its head toward her. Red eyes darted to the hem of her father's jacket, hanging over the side of the boat. It placed its enormous snout on the fabric and breathed deep. Slowly, it raised its head and locked eyes with Jocelyn, dark pupils growing wide.

Terror struck Jocelyn like a physical force. She faltered, dropping her sword to the bottom of the boat. What was she thinking? A girl, not even fully grown, against a colossal crocodile? She didn't stand a chance.

"Captain?" Smee's voice trembled, his eyes wide with fright. "Do you have orders for us?"

Jocelyn sat frozen with terror and doubt, dumbly watching the beast. It did not take its eyes off her.

Smee wrapped his arms about himself. He rocked back and forth. "No. Please," he wept. "Not again! I can't bear it."

At the other end of the boat, Jack began to panic. "Do something!" he screamed. "We've got to get away!" There was nowhere to hide. He stood, flailing his arms. Lantern light bounced off the walls. The boat rocked dangerously in the water.

Jocelyn could not look away. The crocodile was going to eat her. She would die as her father had.

With a speed that seemed impossible, the beast thrust itself out of the water, its dreadful jaws gaping wide. The dinghy tilted, nearly capsizing. Jack stumbled over his seat, sprawling in front of Jocelyn, his lantern hand flung over the side. With a sickening crunch, the lamp was gone—as was most of Jack's arm.

The gruesome scene was illuminated now only by a bit of moonlight, pale and thin as an invalid, creeping through the cave opening.

Jocelyn screamed. Smee swore. Jack let out a mighty shriek of—

You may expect that his wails would be filled with pain, horror, or despair, but as I have come to expect, you would be wrong. In my studies, I've learned quite a lot about the Neverland's crocodile. It relished *those* sounds. The screams of its victims added layers of intense flavoring to its meals, not unlike the spices your mother uses in her cooking.

However, Jack's screams were not the savory seasoning the beast may have expected, for Jack cried out in *gratitude*. No longer would the fledgling pirate have to pretend. Now, and forever after, One-Armed Jack could proudly live up to his name.

When the maimed man cried out, "Thank you! Oh, thank you, my dear creature!" the crocodile lost its appetite and spit out Jack's arm with a grunt. The lost appendage bobbed once or twice then sank beneath the dark water.

The beast gave Jocelyn one last, chilling look before it too submerged. The ticking grew faint, then disappeared altogether.

Smee fumbled about in the dim light and pulled out his handkerchief. After blowing his nose on it one last time, he bandaged the now truly One-Armed Jack's wound.

Jack kept repeating, "Did you see that? He bit off my arm! Wait till I tell the guys. Nubbins has nothing on me. One little thumb? Whoop-de-doo! I lost my arm, my *whole* arm, to the most fearsome beast the Neverland has ever seen—and I lived to tell the tale."

When Smee informed Jack that he might yet die from infection or worse, the new amputee nearly tipped the boat again by dancing a delighted jig.

At the other end of the dinghy, Jocelyn sat in despair. She had frozen. Because of her inaction, one of her men was horribly injured. Granted, he was ecstatic about his wound, but nonetheless, he could have been killed! The realization made her sick to her stomach. What kind of a pirate captain was she? Her father would have been ashamed.

The girl refused to live with that. She must kill the crocodile, or forever carry the taint of failure. Just outside the cave opening, weak moonlight reflected off a series of small bubbles rising to the water's surface. They had to be from the beast.

She reached for the oars, preparing to take command of the little boat. Without warning, there was an explosive boom. The blast knocked Jocelyn to the floor.

Everything went black.

CHAPTER NINETEEN

A Long, Dark Night

I suppose you are wondering what caused the explosion. From what I have been able to discover, it was clearly Jim McCraig's fault, though he never would admit it. People are stubborn like that sometimes.

When Blind Bart heard the crocodile's ticking heading for open water, he called for someone to fire the cannon. Jim and Nubbins, each eager to man the gun, engaged in a bit of a kerfuffle. Nubbins was quicker with a match and lit the fuse, but in a rush of anger, Jim kicked out with his "wooden" leg and repositioned the cannon. The ball flew toward Salmagundi Island, slamming into the cliff face directly above the cave opening. As dirt and rocks rained down, blocking their captain's exit, Jim McCraig turned to Nubbins and said something that, roughly translated, meant "Nicely done, you beef-witted clod."

True night falls fast in the Neverland. That might not have been much of a concern for Blind Bart, but the other men needed their eyes to be any use in a rescue effort. As much as they wanted to begin clearing the rubble away, they were unable to do so in the dark.

The three crew members, like their captain and ship-mates inside the cave, were forced to wait until morning.

Some fool once said that it is always darkest before the dawn. I contend that it is far darker in the dead of night, particularly if you happen to be trapped in a cave. Even more so if you are unconscious. Now, that's dark.

When Jocelyn came to, she found herself and her men in a precarious situation. The explosion had caused a wall of rock and debris to rain down, sealing the cave off tight as a tomb. When all that rubble hit the water, it created a swell that nearly swamped the little dinghy. Their lantern had been destroyed by the crocodile. They were trapped in the dark.

As men of lesser rank must do in times of crisis, Smee and truly One-Armed Jack looked to their captain for answers. Like all great leaders in times of difficulty, Jocelyn had nothing to offer but platitudes and lies.

"Don't worry, men," she said. "We are not alone in this. Bart, Jim, and Nubbins will surely find a way to free us. Even if they cannot, there is bound to be another way out. We only have to wait for the morning sun to shine down some tunnel or crack." Lest her words be considered kind enough to earn Smee's reproach, she threw in, "So quit your sniveling and stay the course, or I'll have you clapped in irons."

Her men were considerably cheered by the girl's leadership, enough so that Jack was able to drift off to sleep—with the assistance of a healthy dose from Smee's emergency grog bottle (for medicinal purposes, of course). Smee had a few gulps himself, then sat in silence. Jocelyn took comfort from nothing, spending a cold, miserable night wrapped in the bitter embrace of failure.

"You know, miss," Smee said, breaking the stillness, "at one time that devil was a regular old crocodile, just like any other. It seemed to me the beast started to change after eating the dear old captain's hand." Smee spoke with a far greater lucidity than he had anytime since Jocelyn had met him. "The captain was more important to me than anything. I left behind family and friends to sail with him, and never regretted it. Why, I'd have flung even Johnny Corkscrew to the sea if he'd asked me to—but don't tell Johnny that. I don't want to hurt his feelings. . . .

"The captain, I lived to serve him, though he did have his faults. He tended toward the melancholies, sometimes not leaving his cabin for weeks, but I was there to see him through. And to be sure, he could get into murderous rages, but he never murdered me. Not once. That's saying something, isn't it?"

"I suppose so," Jocelyn muttered. She wasn't much in a mood to learn about her father's virtues, not with her failure so fresh.

"There was never anyone more wicked than Captain Hook. Never. And that's the way he liked it. But after the crocodile ate his hand, the beast started to get a mite wicked as well. It got bigger and meaner, and, much like the captain, it starting causing more fear than some might think altogether reasonable. Looked to me that no one felt the effects of that strange terror more keenly than the captain himself."

"Why do you think that is?" Jocelyn asked.

"I've been trying to puzzle it out, and to my way of thinking, it goes to reason that some of the captain's great malice might've seeped into the creature when it first had a taste of him. Now that it has had so much more..."

He trailed off, but Jocelyn could grasp his meaning.

Now the beast was truly a monster.

CHAPTER TWENTY

Wherein We Meet Dirty Bob

Though Jocelyn had long despaired of it happening, morning eventually came, and with it a means of escape. As she had surmised, a bit of light forced its way into the cave through a narrow passage in a low area of the ceiling. Though it proved a bit difficult for the portly Mr. Smee, the three were able to wriggle through into the dazzling light of early day.

As she waited for her eyes to adjust, Jocelyn allowed her other senses to take stock of her surroundings. She smelled the earthy scent of dirt mingled with a sweetness of flowers. The morning sun wrapped her in a warm embrace, thawing the stiffness from her cold and tired muscles. Ocean waves crashed in the distance. A nearby bird called to another, "Mildred, dear, could you send over a cup of worms with my Jeffrey? I am fresh out and won't be going to market until later today."

Jocelyn never ceased to be surprised and delighted with the Neverland. If she hadn't been feeling so wretched about her failure with the crocodile, she might have done something foolish, like prance about in the sunshine, gathering wildflowers.

Fortunately, her misery kept her grounded.

Still, the scents, sensations, and sounds made for a pleasant scene, which is why, I suppose, when Jocelyn's eyes did adjust to the brilliance, she was unprepared to be looking down the barrel of a strange man's musket.

I'm going to interrupt my narrative here to inform you that the man holding the musket was ugly, and dirty, and likely full of both vermin and lies. You would be wise not to trust him.

"If Krueger sent ye three misfits to finish me off," the stranger said, "he might be a bit overconfident in your abilities."

Smee pulled Johnny from his sheath and brandished it, his pirate brogue much thicker than usual: "Ye'll pay fer insultin' me cap'n, ye filthy, stinkin' bilge rat! Johnny Corkscrew'll tickle yer liver!"

The man turned to Smee and cried, "So it is true, then, eh? Ye sail under the black flag of Cap'n Krueger?

You'll die for your choice of loyalties! Tell me who this Johnny Corkscrew is, and once I finish with you two ladies and the Lilliput, I'll split him from stem to stern! Where is he?"

Jocelyn drew her own weapon and stepped in front of her loyal bo'sun. "Lower your musket, you filthy dog, or wish that you had."

One-Armed Jack also jumped into the fray. "How would you like some of this?" he shouted, wildly waving his poorly bandaged stump in the man's face.

The stranger lowered his weapon and gave a hearty laugh. "I don't know who captains ye blokes, but I know fer sure it ain't Cap'n Krueger! With the exception of the little girl, he'd not let the likes of you clean the slime off his boots. Of course, that's Minnie's job, but even so... I do like your spunk. I'm Dirty Bob Bonny; what brings you to my island?"

"Humph." Jocelyn sniffed and turned her back on the man. She commanded Jack to find a shady place near the shore and keep an eye out for the ship. Then, addressing Smee, she said, "We need to build a signal fire. Bart will smell the smoke and come round to pick us up."

Dirty Bob clapped his hands together. "Are you telling me, girlie, that you've a ship nearby?"

Jocelyn started pulling dead limbs from a nearby tree. "No. I'm not telling you that. I'm telling my man, Smee."

"Smee, eh? You wouldn't happen to be the same Mr. Smee that sailed under my old mate Hook's flag, would you?" As he asked, Dirty Bob began to help gather wood—certainly for his own selfish reasons.

Jocelyn put down the branch she was holding. "You knew Captain Hook?"

Smee cut off Dirty Bob's reply. "We knew him too, didn't we, Johnny? No one knew the captain better than us."

Jocelyn gave him a comforting kick to the shins. "Of course not, Smee, but just now I want to hear what this man has to say." She resumed gathering branches but told the stranger, "Go on."

"Aye. Ol' Jimmy and me sailed together a long time ago. Course, he wasn't *Captain* then. *Hook* neither, for that matter. That name came a bit later, after he pummeled the cook half to death with his mighty right fist. Didn't much care for raisins in his mush."

"I knew about the raisins," Smee muttered, but Jocelyn shushed him.

Dirty Bob added some dry brush to the woodpile, pulled out a flint and steel, and started the signal fire. "Jim began to be known for fightin', or more to the point, for his powerful right hook. The nickname stuck. Strange, the way he ended up trading that fist for an actual hook…What might your interest in him be?"

"He is—he *was*—my father."

"Well, girlie, I might've guessed you belonged to Hook. You favor him."

Jocelyn fairly glowed with pride. No one had ever told her that before, at least not in a flattering way. "So, if you knew my father when he was young, why didn't you stay with him when he bought his first ship?"

Dirty Bob laughed. "*Bought?* Ah, girlie, Jim never bought a thing in his life. He cheated and murdered his way up the corporate rigging to become bo'sun to Blackbeard himself. Quite an accomplishment, really, but Hook would never be content with anything less than full command. At his first opportunity he betrayed the cap'n, took possession of the *Queen Anne's Revenge*, renamed it the *Jolly Roger*, and there you have it: Hook was no longer subject to anyone. I'd've gone with him if I hadn't a been doing a turn in the stocks."

"That wouldn't a stopped me!" Smee fairly growled at the miscreant.

Jocelyn threatened to send her bo'sun off to sit with One-Armed Jack if he couldn't be quiet. She added more brush to the fire, creating large smoky clouds. "What happened after that, Dirty Bob?"

"Not much of anything. I lost touch with Jim, though I did follow news of his reign of terror some. Impressive. But after a while, he jus' seemed to disappear. As for me, I fell on hard times, drifting around for a few years and bragging that I used to sail with the great Cap'n Hook.

After a time, I met up with Cap'n Krueger. If there's a fouler, greedier, or uglier man on earth, you're not likely to meet him."

The column of smoke drifted up into the sky. Blind Bart was certain to smell it. Jocelyn sat down to wait, and Dirty Bob joined her. Smee remained standing so as to better keep his eye on the man.

"Who is this Captain Krueger?" Jocelyn asked.

Smee spoke up again. "I know! Krueger's a bad one, miss. They say he's got a long white scar down his cheek from a knife fight with a witch woman. Krueger won, but they say that afore she died, the witch cursed him with the gold fever—didn't she, Johnny?"

"My name's not Johnny," Dirty Bob said, "but what you say is true. The curse made Krueger go mad. His unholy need for gold even led him to pull out his own teeth for their gold fillings, replacing them with razor-sharp points from the mouth of a baby shark."

The hair on the back of Jocelyn's neck stood on end. She was struck with an insane desire to see this Krueger up close.

Dirty Bob went on. "I met him one day at a local establishment. I stopped in to get something to quench my thirst, and I guess I must've been a bit verbose about me days with ol' Jim. I don't rightly recall, but I may have stretched the truth a little. Somehow Cap'n Krueger got the idea that I might know something about Hook's treasure."

"Do you?" Jocelyn asked.

"Not rightly, no. But Krueger is obsessed with finding it. He thought I might be able to find Hook's map, so he hired me on his crew. I kept up the charade as long as I could, for he gave a fairly good rum ration, but in the end he came to understand that I didn't know anything. That's when he marooned me on this godforsaken island. I'd been here about three weeks, give or take a year, when you showed up."

Dirty Bob took a silver pocket watch from inside his jacket and began to wind it. Its ticktock grated on Jocelyn's nerves. All the talk about her father's history and his treasure had distracted her from thoughts of the crocodile, but the watch brought them all back. She had to get off the island soon, before the monster got too far away.

As if he could sense her impatience from down the beach, One-Armed Jack jumped up, waving his one arm around and pointing at white sails on the horizon. The *Hook's Revenge* was on the way.

Dirty Bob also spotted the ship growing larger as it neared. "That's me whole story. Now, if you'll have me, I'd love to sign on to your crew. Even as a lad I knew more than most grown men about living the pirate life—and

I've learned a good sight since. Maybe your boys could benefit from my experience."

Jocelyn considered his offer. At times her crew acted more like overgrown children than bloodthirsty pirates. Though for the most part she enjoyed their company, it would be nice to have a more experienced man on board.

Smee tried to argue in favor of leaving Dirty Bob on the island until he rotted—in order to build character. "What kind of example would he be to the men, miss, if he was to give up on being marooned so easily? A quitter, that's what he is."

Jocelyn made up her own mind. She spit on her hand and held it out to Dirty Bob. "Welcome to my crew, Bob. How do you feel about crocodile hunting?"

CHAPTER TWENTY-ONE

*Another Party, Considerably
Less Festive than the First*

From time to time, when I was a younger man, I would return from sea for a brief visit with my family. Those times I came home to find they had thrown a party were always a surprise—to them.

How my parents hated when my unexpected arrival put a damper on their festivities.

When Jocelyn returned with her men to the *Hook's Revenge*, she found that Nubbins was nearly finished preparing a celebratory feast. In *her* honor. How strange.

If the girl was hardly in the mood for a party, she was the only one. The men attacked their food with gusto, noisily sucking their fingers and belching loud enough to rattle the trenchers. They sang while they ate, spewing bits of half-chewed meat all over the table. When a Loudest Flatulence contest broke out, Jocelyn excused herself to the far end of the galley, where she sat alone. She almost missed the quiet dining hall at Miss Eliza's.

Mr. Smee joined her. "Your mum didn't like pirate feasts all that much either."

The empty place in Jocelyn's heart sat up and began paying attention. "Is that why she left my father?"

Smee wriggled in his seat. "I'm not supposed—"

"Mr. Smee, as your captain, I order you to tell me what you know about my mother."

"But miss—"

"Spill it, you dirty, stinking bilge rat!"

Smee beamed at her. "Aye, Captain, thank you, sir! Your mum—lovely girl, she was. She looked a gentle-woman through and through, but she was a pirate at the core. Who else could have stolen the captain's heart?"

That was certainly not how Sir Charles had ever described his daughter. To hear her grandfather speak, Evelina had been as perfect and pure as a newborn baby angel.

"I believe they truly were happy. For a while, anyways. But then came the end. It was the same old story. The captain never did care much for high society teas, and though we couldn't understand it, Miss Evelina got tired of plunder and murder. She left for home with a small bit of pirate's gold in her purse and . . . well, a surprise of sorts. You were born later that year."

Smee and Jocelyn lapsed into thoughtfulness. Their silence was broken by One-Armed Jack, whose lusty retelling of the adventure in the cave went awry when he tripped over his own feet and landed in Smee's lap. Jack didn't miss a beat, jumping up and continuing his tale, but when he got to the part where Jocelyn froze, he paused, looking confused. "Cap'n, what *did* happen back there?" he asked. "Why didn't you strike the monster?"

"None of your business, you stinking codfish! I am the captain—how dare you question me?"

Smee looked fit to burst with pride. "That's telling him, miss! You're shaping up to be every bit a captain as your old dad. If you want me to get out the cat-o'-nine, just say the word."

Before the men could start lining up for their chance to be lashed, Jocelyn stormed off to the main deck. There she stood, alone at the bow, thinking about the crocodile. Jocelyn recalled being in the dinghy, sword at the ready, victory in her sights and then . . . it all fell apart.

For the briefest of moments she thought she heard the faint ticking of a clock, but then the wind changed direction and carried the sound away.

She opened her locket and looked at her father's picture. "I am trying so hard to be the kind of captain you were, but how can I do what you could not?" she whispered. "Perhaps I'm not exactly suited for pirating, like my mother." But if Jocelyn couldn't be a pirate, what would she do?

A tear fell on her locket, landing on her father's face. It was quite possibly the first to be present there. It looked absurd on his cheek. Jocelyn dried the locket on her sleeve and snapped it closed. Wiping her eyes with the back of her hand, she looked to the horizon. Somewhere out there, the beast lurked.

It had stolen her father from her. It had made her look foolish in front of her men. It was a monster, a danger to anyone it came in contact with. The girl gathered her resolve. One failure may have rattled her, but she would not surrender.

Time was running out for the crocodile.

I've found that, occasionally, a good cry is really all that is needed. They don't even have to be my own tears to be therapeutic. Making another person miserable enough to hiccup and sob generally does the trick for me, but to each his own.

After taking a few moments to compose herself, Jocelyn returned to the galley to find her somewhat subdued men getting acquainted with Dirty Bob. With the exception of Mr. Smee (who surely knew better than to be taken in by the braggart's fancy talk), the crew fawned over him like a bunch of starry-eyed schoolgirls.

"Is it true you were marooned? You lucky devil!"

"Can you explain exactly what 'bucko' means?"

"Tell us about your days sailing with Hook! What was he really like?"

That last question was a particular affront to poor Mr. Smee. He muttered quietly to Johnny, "Why, we sailed with the captain for years. Who knows him better than his own bo'sun? No one, that's who."

Jocelyn smoothed his ruffled feathers by asking for advice. "Mr. Smee, I have unfinished business with the crocodile. It is clear that none of the other men know how to find it, but I have a feeling you might be able to come up with something that will help."

"Of course, of course. Let me think...." He removed his spectacles and polished them on the hem of his shirt. As he had recently employed his hem as a replacement for his handkerchief, they came up quite a bit dirtier than before. "Let's see... Tiger Lily, the Indian princess, might have warriors of some sort that can track the beast for us. We could kidnap her and force her to help us."

"Excellent idea, Smee, though I'm not sure kidnapping is in order. Perhaps we can simply ask her for help?"

"*Ask* her? I don't know, miss. The captain would've kidnapped her. Asking doesn't seem to be very sporting."

"All right, then, kidnapping it is. Polish the manacles and let's be on our way."

Like a puppy seeking attention, the main island of the Neverland crept closer during the night. If the girl hadn't already planned her return, she likely would have found the entire landmass wriggling in her lap, begging for a belly rub. Instead of days, the return voyage took no more than a few hours.

Jocelyn explained to the men that she would be leading an expedition to Tiger Lily's village. "Mr. Smee will accompany. Are there any other volunteers?"

She expected them to jump at a chance for more adventures, but only Dirty Bob stepped forward. The rest of the men stared at the deck.

"What is the matter with you dogs?" she snapped. "I thought you were thirsting for adventure!"

One-Armed Jack answered. "Um, Cap'n? We can't go. Her village is too close to Peter's camp."

"Whose camp?" Jocelyn asked.

"Don't you know Peter Pan, the leader of the lost boys?"

"That irritating flying boy? What does he have to do with anything?" Jocelyn asked.

Jack shuffled his feet. "We haven't gone anywhere near his camp, Cap'n—not since we were boys. We've been banished."

CHAPTER TWENTY-TWO

In Which Something Lost Is Found

Stop gawking and close your mouth before I decide to use it as a trash receptacle.

Yes, yes, it's true. Jocelyn's fierce, fighting pirates were nothing more than banished lost boys, all grown up.

As such, they couldn't come with Jocelyn, but remembering the havoc they'd caused with the cannon, she didn't feel comfortable leaving them alone. She commanded Dirty Bob to stay behind and keep an eye on things. Because they were now down to two dinghies, after the loss of the first in the cave, Smee rowed her to shore in the spare, tying it at Plunder Point. From there it would be only a short walk through the forest to Tiger Lily's village.

Though it felt like a pleasant spring day, the trees and ground were dusted with white. Jocelyn reached down and grabbed a handful of snow. She expected it to be warm, like the snowflakes had been in her dream, but it was as cold and dull as English snow. She dropped it in disgust.

"What's the matter, miss?" Smee asked.

"Nothing," she said as she wiped her hand on her jacket. "I just thought the snow would be warm."

Smee laughed. "Warm, she says! Warm snow on the ground. Have you ever heard such a thing, Johnny?"

Jocelyn scowled at him. "I don't see what's so funny. This island is full of surprises. Why not warm snow?"

"Of course it's warm when it falls, but the longer it sits, the colder it gets—like when you're called to dinner and you don't come in right away." Smee stuck his finger in a snowbank. "This here has been sitting out all night or longer. It's stone cold now." He pulled his finger out, sticking it in his armpit to remove the icy sting. "Oh, and it probably goes without saying, but mayhaps I should remind you: if you see any snow lizards, don't pick them up, unless you want to get yourself frostbit." Smee continued chuckling as he ambled up the path. Jocelyn followed, keeping an eye out for the cold-blooded creatures.

If her expedition had been planned in order to explore the Neverland and see some of its creatures, it would have been a raging success. In addition to snow lizards, she spied a pair of brown-faced gnomes, a large herd of pooka, and the uncommon bare-fronted hoodwink.

Jocelyn almost resolved to take time to explore, simply for the sake of exploring, once she finished with the crocodile, but then she thought of her father. He would not have been likely to go on a nature expedition unless there was blood or treasure at stake. When the girl saw a red-feathered serpent sunning itself on a rock, she made a point to yawn at it, set her face toward the Indian village, and march on.

A short while later they arrived at Tiger Lily's camp, only to find it deserted—populated with empty tipi frames and cold fire pits.

"Begging your pardon, miss," Smee said, "but it looks like they've gone on the hunt. There's no telling when they'll return."

Jocelyn could not believe their terrible luck. She had no idea how to find the crocodile now. There was nothing to do but return to the ship. This task proved to be rather difficult as well, for when they got back to Plunder Point, they found that their spare dinghy had been chopped full of holes. A dull ax lay in a patch of nearby sea grass. Clearly, this was the work of Peter Pan or his lost boys.

Jocelyn felt certain that Blind Bart would hear them and send the spare-spare if they called out for him to do so, but Smee insisted on swimming back for it while she waited. She didn't have the heart to argue.

Jocelyn sat with her back to a tree and threw rocks at the useless boat. They made a satisfying bang as they crashed against its wooden sides.

The whole day had been so infuriating!

Bang!

A useless hike. No warriors. And now this.

Bang! Bang!

What a stupid waste of time!

Thud.

"Ow! Come on, fellas, we're under attack!" a boyish voice called out.

In her anger, Jocelyn had pitched the last rock wild. It had discovered its target in an overgrown berry patch beyond the boat. Before she could even get to her feet, Jocelyn found herself being pelted with a volley of over-ripe blackberries. Sticky, purple juice stained her face and body.

"Stop that this instant!" she commanded.

The berries immediately stopped raining down on Jocelyn.

"Did you hear that, Ace?"

"I heard it. Did you hear it, Fredo?"

"Yeah. It sounded like a girl. What do you think, Twin?"

"Sure did. How about you, Dodge? Hey, where's Dodge?"

"I think he went to pick more berries. We used all the mushiest ones from this bush."

While this conversation went on, Jocelyn crept closer to the berry patch. After parting the foliage, she saw four dirty-faced boys crouched on the other side. They smelled of camp smoke and were dressed in animal skins. Jocelyn had found the lost boys.

"I thought that was a pirate's rowboat. What's a girl doing with a pirate, Fredo?" asked a small boy dressed in jackalope fur. He didn't seem to notice that his antlers were tangled in the brambles.

A chubby boy wearing a too-small jacket, pieced together from squirrel skins, answered him. "Perhaps she has been captured. We should rescue her."

"Yes, let's, Fredo!" agreed a pair of boys dressed alike in skunk shirts and hats, long black and white tails dangling down their backs. "Won't Peter be pleased with us?"

Jocelyn wrinkled her nose, as much at the mention of that cocky boy as at the ripe scent coming off the boys' furs. "Look here," she said. "I've already gone over this with your Peter what's-his-name. I don't need rescuing."

The boys hardly looked at Jocelyn. They went on with their discussion as if she weren't there. "The girl said she didn't need rescuing, Ace."

Jackalope shrugged. "That's what I thought she said, Fredo. I wonder why not, Twin."

"I don't know. Let's ask Dodge when he gets—"

"You two are twins? And both . . . named Twin?" Jocelyn interrupted. Aside from their skunk-skin clothes, the two boys couldn't have looked more different. One was short with freckles and ginger hair and the other tall and dark-skinned. "You don't look anything alike."

"Yes we do," the smaller twin said.

"Peter said so—right, Ace?" the larger twin continued.

Ace nodded, shaking the bush with his tangled jackalope horns. "Right, Twin. Peter said we need twins. You two got the short straws, so you are it." He pointed at each boy in turn. "Twin and Twin."

"That's right, Ace," the skunk boys replied in unison.

"Oh, Peter said so, did he?" Jocelyn really disliked that boy. "Of all the stupid—ouch! What was that?" Jocelyn felt it again, a sharp tug on the back of her head, ripping out several hairs. She slapped at whatever it was that was attacking her, but missed.

The chubby boy laughed. "You'll never catch her like that; she's too quick."

A streak of light flashed across the girl's vision. "Who's too quick? What was that?"

"She's Peter's fairy, Tinker Bell," the tall twin said.

"Tink doesn't like girls much," the short one added.

"I can see that," Jocelyn replied as the fairy gave her a pinch on the back of her leg. "Can you get her to stop?"

"I dunno; we've never tried," the chubby boy said. "Tink. Stop." The fairy ripped a button from Jocelyn's jacket and hurled it to the ground. "I guess not."

"Not for a lack of effort, I'm sure," Jocelyn said. "What does she have against girls?"

"She's either jealous that they like Peter—"

"Or angry that they don't. Right, Dodge?" The twins addressed someone behind Jocelyn. She turned in time to be hit full in the face with a handful of rotten berries.

"Right!" the new voice replied.

Jocelyn wiped juice from her eyes, trying to get a better look at the berry flinger.

The boy stood in front of her—dressed not in skins but in dirty and torn clothing, with burs in his curly hair and streaks of dried mud on his face—sporting a very familiar grin. Jocelyn could hardly believe her eyes.

"Roger?"

CHAPTER TWENTY-THREE

The Lost Boy

It can be disconcerting to meet a familiar person someplace unexpected. Jocelyn's situation brings to mind the time I found my neighbor's gardener digging behind the church. Of course, finding a gardener turning up earth is not out of the ordinary. However, it was past midnight *and* in a graveyard. He startled me so much that I dropped my shovel.

If Jocelyn had been holding a shovel, she would have dropped it as well. She rushed toward her friend, pulling him into a hug. As boys that age are wont to do, he squirmed out of her embrace and threw another berry at her. Perhaps because Jocelyn was showing such interest in someone other than Peter, the fairy ceased her attack and settled on a leaf to watch.

"Oh, Roger, I can't believe it!" Jocelyn said. "Today was absolutely the worst day. I felt like giving up, but then I turned around and here you are. Edgar must have brought you back with him after he delivered my letter. Isn't the Neverland wonderful? What adventures we will have together, just like you promised!"

Roger didn't reply. Jocelyn felt a sinking in her stomach. Why was he just standing there staring at her? Certainly he hadn't come all this way to tell her he was angry with her about being sent away from the school.

"Roger?" A world of questions hung on that single word. His reply left every one of them unanswered.

"I'm Dodge," he said. "What's your name?"

Behind her, the other lost boys started giggling. "Did you hear what she called him, Ace?"

"I heard her, what about you, Fredo?"

Jocelyn ignored them, peering into Roger's brown eyes. They looked different somehow—vacant, and lacking the sparkle she was used to. "Don't you know who I am? It's me, Jocelyn."

"That's a nice name. I like it. Did Peter bring you here too?"

Ugh, him again. "Peter? That flying boy brought you? How did—"

Mention of Peter got the fairy's attention. Jocelyn felt another sharp pinch, this one to her ear. The little devil rang out a series of alarm bells and wagged a tiny finger in Jocelyn's face before flying back to her leaf.

Jocelyn rubbed at her sore earlobe, considering her phrasing. "I would like to know how you got here."

"I told you: Peter brought me. I was running away from the workhouse——"

"Workhouse? What were you doing there?"

Workhouses are bleak establishments created to give the poor yet another reason to feel miserable. Picturing Roger in one of those awful places made Jocelyn's heart ache. "Were those the 'other arrangements' Miss Eliza made for you?"

"I don't know. I just remember that I had been there for a short time and I was leaving. Before that, I really can't recall. A boy, Peter Pan, landed in front of me and asked if I wanted to have adventures. Who could refuse? Did he bring you too?"

"No, Pet—" Jocelyn noticed the fairy glaring and shaking her head. "Er, *that person* did not bring me here! I came on my own to hunt the Neverland crocodile. When I saw you, I thought—I hoped—you were here to help me."

The other lost boys' giggles turned into full-on laughs. "That girl says she's going to fight the crocodile, Twin," the chubby boy said.

Before either twin could answer, Jocelyn turned around and shoved the closest boy, the one in jackalope fur. He fell to the ground, tearing his hood on the brambles.

"I've had enough out of all of you. Get out of here before I lose my temper."

The fairy made a laughing sort of tinkling sound and fell off her leaf. She got up with a red face and flew away, but not before she gave Jocelyn one last pinch. Jackalope Boy picked himself up and dusted his backside. "All right, all right, we're going. You coming, Dodge?"

Roger frowned. "In a minute. I want to talk to this girl some more."

The boys shook their heads at him but didn't argue.

"Roger," Jocelyn said, once they were out of sight, "don't you remember anything from before you went to the workhouse?"

He squinted his eyes and tapped his head. "I remember . . . something about an explorer, with a funny name—Madge Allen, I think. He might have been a lost boy once."

"That's right, Magellan. But he wasn't a lost boy. We read about him on the day before my birthday. Remember that night? We looked at the stars and you gave me a gift—well, actually more of a loan—but I've kept it with me ever since. Here, I'll give it back to you now." She reached for her pocket.

"Is it a kiss? Peter told us girls like to give kisses. I think I should like to have one."

Jocelyn's hand froze. Her face grew hot. "You want, er, a . . ."

In fairy tales, a kiss had the power to break an enchantment. Perhaps...

She looked again into her friend's eyes. They showed nothing but mild curiosity. He held out a hand to receive her "kiss." Roger had no idea what he was asking for. Jocelyn was struck with a desire to either punch him or sob.

Ignoring both impulses, she dug the little brass compass from her pocket and slapped it into his outstretched palm. "No, Roger, it was this." Her voice softened. "Doesn't it look familiar? It was your father's."

He held the compass close to his face and examined it. "My father's... He was lost, wasn't he? Was *he* a lost boy?"

Jocelyn felt tears welling up behind her eyes. Why couldn't he remember anything? "No, he wasn't a lost boy. He was lost at sea. Can you remember him?"

For the first time, the girl wondered what *had* happened to Roger's father. With dawning dismay, she considered the possibility that pirates, perhaps even her own father, might have had something to do with his death. The weight of that realization added to the guilt Jocelyn already carried over Roger's dismissal.

"Lost at sea..." Roger stared out at the ocean as if he might be able to find his father there. Jocelyn's eyes followed his gaze. Mr. Smee was returning in the spare-spare dinghy.

"Listen, Roger," she said, "you can come with me, back to my ship. I'll help you remember." He didn't look at her, but gripped the compass hard in his fist.

"A pirate is in the harbor!" shouted one of the boys. "Come on, Dodge, we've got to tell Peter!" Without a word, Roger turned away.

"Roger!" Jocelyn called to him.

He turned back, giving her his jolliest grin. "Good luck with the crocodile, girl," he called, and, pocketing the compass, ran after the other boys. Jocelyn watched, brokenhearted, as her friend disappeared into the trees.

Roger truly was a lost boy. Jocelyn had been the one to lose him.

CHAPTER TWENTY-FOUR

Killing Time

Losing is painful. Whether it be a friend, a gold piece, or the tip of your little finger, loss hurts in a way that most other things do not.

Jocelyn hardly noticed Smee's return. She sat on the ground, knees drawn up and arms around them.

"Don't worry, Miss Captain," he said. "I brought back a marlinspike and a belaying pin. We'll find those rotten children that messed up the spare and teach them a lesson or two."

Jocelyn shook her head and climbed into the boat.

"But miss! We can't just leave it be, can we? That's not the way it's done. They attack us and we attack back. It's the pirate way."

"Sorry, Smee, I'm not in the mood. Let's go back to the ship."

"And now you've gone and said sorry to me! Did the captain ever say he was sorry to any of his men? No! And you—"

"Mr. Smee," Jocelyn cried, "I am *not* my father and I never will be! Take me back to my ship."

Smee snapped his mouth closed and started rowing. After a few strokes, he recovered his wits and prattled on about getting revenge on Peter and the lost boys. Jocelyn hardly noticed. She wrapped her father's jacket tight around her but received no warmth from it.

Over the sound of the wind, the waves, and Smee's muttering, Jocelyn heard ticking. A trail of bubbles followed along behind the boat. She braced herself to fight, but the crocodile never surfaced. Instead, the bubbles disappeared and the sound died. She whipped her head from side to side, searching the water, but there was nothing there.

The beast appeared to be toying with her. Jocelyn's nerves were stretched nearly to the breaking point— perhaps that was its intention. And her meeting with Roger certainly hadn't helped things.

Roger. How could he have forgotten her? Could it be that he didn't want to remember? Certainly they had been friends at school, but it wasn't as if he had been given other options. He'd practically said as much. His only choices had been her or Cook. Perhaps since Jocelyn didn't smell like onions . . .

But then she'd gotten him fired—and sent to the workhouse. The workhouse! She couldn't imagine a more terrible place. Even worse than that, her own father might have been part of the reason Roger had become an orphan. Why on earth would he want to remember her?

Back aboard the *Hook's Revenge*, she pulled Blind Bart aside. "Did you hear the beast? Is it still nearby?"

"I most certainly did, Captain Jocelyn, though the sound of its internal timepiece is no longer present. The crocodile must be far from us now."

"And before? When I was with the lost boys?" Jocelyn's face reddened. "I assume you heard all of that as well?"

"Why yes, I was an unfortunate party to your trouble. My hearing is so fine—"

"Yes, I know, it's marvelous, but we are not talking about you right now. Since you heard it all anyway, I'll ask you: Why do lost boys forget?"

Bart scratched his head. "Interesting question. There are multiple theories regarding the amnesia manifested in the denizens of the Neverland."

"Just give me the most likely. In simple terms, please."

Blind Bart sighed and adjusted his eye patches. "It's part of the magic of the Neverland. Forgetting keeps you from growing up."

"Then why do I still remember everything?"

"Why indeed?" Blind Bart asked, then nodded and walked away.

Jocelyn considered the question. It would be lovely to forget all the failures and disappointments she had encountered over the past few days, but where would that get her? She'd be stuck in one place, forever. Jocelyn did not want to always remain the same. Where was the adventure in that?

Still, it would be nice to forget Roger as cleanly and neatly as he had forgotten her. At least then it wouldn't hurt so much.

That night, for the second time in her life, Jocelyn dreamed of her father. On this occasion he walked along beside her in the dark. She knew that they were following the crocodile, but they were traveling in a big loop. Round and round the circle they went. It grew difficult to tell who was following whom. Were they hunting the monster, or was it hunting them?

Jocelyn tried asking her father what he thought, but he would not reply. No matter what she did, he was unable to see her. She stopped and grabbed him by the arm, forcing him to face her. "Look at me!" she cried. "Tell me what to do!"

Captain Hook finally turned his eyes on the girl, but when he opened his mouth to speak, only ticking came out. Beneath her fingers, his arm lost shape, turning into hard reptilian armor. Bloodred eyes shone in the darkness. The sound of a clock filled her head. The beast snarled and opened wide its wicked mouth. Jocelyn could do nothing to stop it.

It was going to eat her.

She woke in a cold sweat, tangled in bedsheets. Her arms flailed, fumbling for her sword. The infernal ticktock still filled the air. It was present in her head, in her cabin, aboard her ship.

Jocelyn dazedly pulled herself from the jumble of blankets. She felt as if she were still in a dream, as if she were somehow an observer of the scene rather than a participant. In the mirror above her mantel, her unblinking eyes reflected an eerie red light. She turned away and opened her cabin door, gliding across the deck like an apparition, feet bare, tattered white nightgown flapping in the breeze.

Dirty Bob was on duty. He stood gazing out at the darkness, fiddling with his pocket watch. Its ticking marred the stillness of the night. Like a destroying angel, Jocelyn advanced upon the man, her sword upheld.

He turned. "Good evening, Cap'n..." Bob's eyes met hers and his voice trailed off.

Jocelyn lunged, slashing with her sword. She cleanly severed the chain securing his pocket watch, and it fell with a dull thud to the deck. She attacked with a fury, hacking and smashing, until the timepiece lay broken, scattered, and silent.

Dirty Bob gathered up the bits and put them back in his pocket. He turned a sad eye on Jocelyn and said, "That watch was the first thing I ever stole."

The girl's heart cried out with remorse, but the image of her father was still with her. "I'll have no ticking aboard my ship," she said before retreating to her cabin and slamming the door.

If you ask me, Dirty Bob likely deserved the attack upon his property. He did *not* deserve an apology note accompanied by Captain Hook's own sterling-silver double cigar holder, but apparently Jocelyn felt otherwise the next morning.

CHAPTER TWENTY-FIVE

The Flying Dutchman

Jocelyn spent much of the next day alone in her cabin. Smee brought her meals, but they went untouched. However, being young and not much used to the blackness of depression, she found that her stamina for self-pity petered out by dinnertime. She joined her crew in time to hear Dirty Bob, gleefully smoking dual cigars, tell a tale about the *Flying Dutchman*.

Given your general lack of knowledge concerning anything of interest, I'll assume you know nothing about the *Dutchman*. The short version is this: The *Flying Dutchman* is a ghost ship doomed to sail on forever. She is almost always accompanied by a storm that appears from nowhere. Those unlucky enough to see the cursed vessel generally meet with an early doom. They might be washed overboard, killed in drunken brawls, or struck with dysentery. One unfortunate sailor I know of fell over the railing and was eaten alive by a pod of passing dolphins.

Dirty Bob's story went late, well into first watch. Still feeling remorse over her behavior the night before, Jocelyn excused her men, taking the post herself. However, thanks to Bob's storytelling, the crew members were too afraid to be alone in their bunks. They all crowded around the girl "so that she wouldn't be lonely."

Jim McCraig with a Wooden Leg made his way to the young captain through the press of bodies. Smee translated: "Captain, I feel the phantom ache. Storm's coming."

Nubbins broke into a panic. "A storm's coming? It's the *Flying Dutchman*. Save us!"

His hysteria spread faster than the pox. One-Armed Jack cried out, "I want my mother!"

The wind changed direction and began to blow with new intensity. Blind Bart made sure his eye patches were in place, invisibility affording him some protection.

The first few drops of rain fell. Smee made a sound that was certainly not a shriek and struggled to hide in an apple barrel.

Lightning flashed. Nubbins knelt down and loudly confessed his sins. (None were worth listening to.)

Thunder rattled the deck. One-Armed Jack cried

out, "I-I-I see it! Lord have mercy, it's the *F-F-Flying Dutchman*!"

Jocelyn climbed upon a crate and whistled for attention. "Stop this foolishness before I give you dogs something to be afraid of! What you are looking at is a thundercloud on the horizon! It is not the *Flying Dutchman*!"

The crew listened, taking courage from her words. Jocelyn continued. "A storm is coming and it may be a bad one. This is no time to lose our heads—we've got to ready the ship. I will not have you all distracted by ghost stories, so I will only say this once: There is no such thing as the *Flying Dutchman*!"

The crew scurried off to batten hatches and secure rigging.

"Strike the sails or they will be ripped to shreds!" Jocelyn called after them. She turned into the gale and faced the gathering clouds, trying to determine the best course of action. Something on the waves caught the girl's attention. She rubbed the lens of her spyglass and held it up for a closer look.

A great black ship was sailing directly out of the storm. If she hadn't seen it with her own eyes, Jocelyn would never have believed it, but there it was, clear as could be: a ghost ship heading right at them.

A part of her wanted to react as Smee had, to run away and find someplace safe (quite sensible of him, if you ask me), but she was the captain. If anyone, living or dead, threatened her ship, she had no choice but to blast them out of the water. Even in her fright, that thought made her smile. This would be ever so much better than paper boats aflame.

Quietly, so as not to attract any attention, she made her way to Dirty Bob. The rest of the men were too busy preparing for the storm to notice. "Bob, I saw the *Dutchman*. It's coming for us. How can we fight it?"

The wind howled as the storm gathered strength. Dirty Bob took Jocelyn's spyglass and looked. "No! It couldn't be. But the ship—it's unmistakable." Bob's hand shook. He lowered the glass and handed it back to the girl. Lightning flashed again, closer this time, and its light illuminated fear on the old pirate's face.

"That's not the *Dutchman*—would that it were! Cap'n, you'd best ready your men for a fight. That there is the *Calypso's Nightmare*, sailed by a man worse'n the devil himself.

"Prepare to meet Captain Krueger."

CHAPTER TWENTY-SIX

Battling Calypso's Nightmare

The *Calypso's Nightmare* and the storm raced to see who would arrive first. In what little time she had left, Jocelyn struggled to ready her crew for their first battle.

"Offer no quarter and take no prisoners!" the girl shouted, but the wind stole her words and flung them away. The sea rose and fell, enormous waves buffeting the ship. Rain poured in earnest now, making the deck slick and treacherous.

Jocelyn ordered Jack to drop anchor. The *Hook's Revenge* slowly turned about, getting into position for firing. Krueger's ship was close now. Even through the deluge, Jocelyn could see his bloodthirsty crew waving pistols and cutlasses in anticipation of fighting. Her untested men didn't stand a chance against them. She called for Jim to fire a warning shot across the bow.

Are you surprised to learn he missed? His shot hit the tip of Kruger's mast. Other than breaking off the flagpole, no damage was sustained.

The loss of their flag only angered the rival pirates. Jocelyn faintly heard their curses over the roaring storm. The *Calypso's Nightmare* was now close enough that the girl could make out an eager wildness in the crew's eyes, and the ship did not appear to be slowing.

"Fire the cannons again! Aim to hit her this time!" Jocelyn yelled.

Jim's shot went wide, dropping harmlessly into the roiling sea.

Jocelyn ran across the deck, desperate to get below and take over the cannon. Pounding waves rocked the ship from side to side; it was difficult to keep her balance. Just as she reached the hatch, Jocelyn heard the *thwock-thwock* of grappling hooks strike her railing. She was too late. The *Hook's Revenge* was about to be boarded.

"They're coming, men! Ready your arms!" she shouted.

One-Armed Jack complained, "That's terribly insensitive, Cap'n. You can't ready your *arms* if you only have one."

Jocelyn glared at him and shouted, "Shut up and get ready to fight, you fool!"

"Aye, aye, Cap'n," he said with a left-handed salute. "A real pirate war? Hurrah!"

The first wave of Krueger's men landed on deck and the battle began. Jocelyn pulled her sword from its sheath and jumped into the fray. A huge man, covered in warts and tattoos, had Blind Bart in a headlock. Even in the dim light Jocelyn could see Bart's face beginning to turn an unhealthy shade of blue. Fearful of damaging her lookout should she try to use her sword, Jocelyn ran up and kicked the warty pirate in . . . well, in an unfair place.

Quit your cringing. It was the right thing to do. Pirates do not fight fair.

The man let go of Bart and doubled over, wheezing. Bart tumbled to the deck, overcome.

Wild with rage, Warty recovered quickly. "You'll pay for that, little miss!" he yelled.

The girl's sword flashed and the big man's speech was cut off—as were his pants. He stood there in his not-so-clean underwear, looking too astonished to move. Jocelyn backed up a few steps to get a better view of the spectacle. Her laughter pealed out, rising above the cacophony of wind and wave.

Grabbing his pants with one hand and his cutlass with the other, the pirate moved toward her. "I'll teach you some manners, girlie."

"That's unlikely. I've already been to finishing school," she replied, her blade at the ready. She took a step toward him and swung. He parried the blow. Their clashing weapons shot sparks that were immediately snuffed out in the rain.

Though he was larger and stronger, Jocelyn was quick. While fending off the man's cutlass with her sword arm, she used her free hand to poke him in the eye. He howled, dropping both his weapon and his pants, and grabbed Jocelyn in a wresting hold, pinning her arms to her sides.

"Fancy a swim, missy?" he growled as he dragged her to the side of the ship.

Jocelyn thrashed and kicked but was unable to free herself. The railing pressed into her back as her feet lifted from the deck. She would be tossed into the stormy sea and drown.

"Stand down, Benito!" a deep voice commanded. A newcomer approached, his face cloaked in shadow.

"But Cap'n—" Warty began, earning him a sharp slap across the face. He dropped Jocelyn to the deck in a heap.

"Now go cut the lines to the lifeboat while I parlay with the little captain here. I wouldn't want anyone to leave before the party is over. And pull up your breeches."

"Aye, aye, Cap'n Krueger, sir."

Jocelyn stood. The deck pitched and yawed under her feet. She steadied herself and brandished her sword. "What right have you to board my ship? I'll gut you for this, Krueger."

Reaching out his index finger, Krueger pushed her

blade down. "Put that away, child, before someone gets hurt. I'm here to parlay—to discuss the terms of your surrender." Lightning flashed, illuminating a long white scar and rows of pointy teeth.

"Why would I surrender to you?"

"Your crew of imbeciles is nothing compared to my trained fighters. Acquiesce to my demands or I will kill every last one of them. Slowly."

Jocelyn glanced around. Blind Bart lay unconscious on the deck. Her other men were holding on, but it was plain to see they were outmatched. She sheathed her sword. "What do you want?"

Lightning flashed again, glinting off Krueger's sharp smile. "Give me the map to Hook's treasure and I will let all of you go."

"I don't have it."

He took a step closer, bending to bring his face close to hers. Jocelyn recoiled at his terrible breath, but with her back to the railing, she had no escape.

"Liar! You are Hook's heir. He left his map to you. You may think the treasure is your rightful inheritance, but you will not get it. That gold belongs to me."

"So sorry to disappoint you," Jocelyn replied in a tone that clearly indicated she was not a bit sorry, "but all my father left me was a nearly impossible task. My only inheritance is to avenge his death on the Neverland's crocodile. Feel free to steal that, if you like."

Krueger pulled back his hand to strike and Jocelyn jerked her face away. At that instant, an enormous wave hit the ship. The deck tilted sharply and Jocelyn lost her balance. She tumbled over the railing to the boiling sea below.

In the chaos of storm and battle, no one even heard a splash.

CHAPTER TWENTY-SEVEN

Drowning—Not as Much Fun as One Might Think

Jocelyn smashed into the icy waves with a force that drove all air from her lungs and pushed her deep under the water's surface. Stunned and disoriented, the girl wasn't even certain which way was up. It was terrifying, so dark and horribly cold. She tried to kick, but her legs were tangled in the long tails of her father's jacket. Jocelyn struggled to get free as though her life depended on it, because, as she full well knew, it did. With a Herculean effort she was able to wrench her arms from the sleeves. Captain Hook's coat sank to the bottom of the sea.

The girl flailed and kicked, fighting for the surface. Something in the water brushed against her face. She reached, barely grasping it in her frantic hands—a rope!

Hand over hand, Jocelyn pulled herself along. It was hard to keep going; her chest burned with the searing, horrific pain of drowning.

Memories darted through her mind as though being performed on her own private stage.

It was Christmastime and Sir Charles had given a ball. How did the ladies manage not to fidget and scratch in their gowns? Her own little dress felt tight and itchy. She wondered, had her mother ever danced with her father like that?

She was at the seashore, a bit older, missing her front teeth. She sat on the sand, trying to make a castle, but she was too close to the water. Even when the tide crept up and destroyed her work, she refused to move. Stamping a foot at the waves, she yelled, "Go away! I was here first!"

She was in a fast carriage heading for another seashore holiday. The countryside raced away, giving the impression that the coach was standing still while the earth moved. Traveling so fast was exciting. Grandfather's warm hand covered hers. He smiled at her.

Jocelyn was tired. So tired. The need for air was unbearable.

At last, quite literally at the end of her rope, Jocelyn's reaching hand grasped solid wood. With indescribable relief, she broke through the surface of the water. She took a deep, shuddering breath, gulping air and more than a little seawater. Her throat burned and head ached, but she was grateful to be alive. She found that she was gripping the edge of her own spare-spare dinghy. Captain Krueger's plan to keep Jocelyn and her crew from escaping the *Hook's Revenge* by pushing the little boat overboard had proved to be her salvation.

It does my heart good to know how much the villain would have hated that.

Jocelyn managed to pull herself in before collapsing from exhaustion. It was several minutes before she regained enough sense to take stock of the situation.

The girl was clearly stranded in the middle of the ocean. She had no food. In the bottom of the boat there was plenty of fresh water from the storm, but if she did not start to bail soon, she would sink. Her jacket was gone; one of her shoes was missing. The storm continued to blow with horrifying force, tossing the dinghy about on immense waves. Such conditions would have made it impossible for Jocelyn to steer even if her oars had not been lost.

On the positive side, by some miracle she had not lost her sword. She still had her wits about her. She was uninjured. And, for the time being, at least, Jocelyn was alive. She would just have to figure out how to stay that way.

CHAPTER TWENTY-EIGHT

Wherein Jocelyn Meets
Three Hideous Beauties

Nothing lasts forever. Just ask any of my ex-wives.

Long before dawn, the storm discovered it was late for an appointment and abruptly left, nearly forgetting its hat in a rush to be elsewhere. Jocelyn fell into a deep slumber, though the poor girl would not be allowed to rest for long.

Three baleful sisters circled her little boat, craning to see what it contained. They were not impressed. "Look at the horrid little thing!" Jocelyn was indeed a sight: damp, dirty, and disheveled, with her dress torn and stockings bunched at her ankles. Exhaustion had given her skin an unhealthy pallor, and her hair was tangled with seaweed.

"It is a pity it did not drown." Although the words

themselves plumbed the depths of ugliness, the voice that spoke was like rain in the desert: sweet and cold.

Peals of laughter rang out in reply.

Jocelyn stirred, wondering at the beauty of the sound. It was possible she was imagining the voices, yet even if they were real, the girl was too exhausted to care. She lay on her back and looked up at the clear night sky, nearly full to bursting with stars. In vain, she tried to locate the North Star. It swam in and out of focus in front of her bleary eyes.

The boat rose and fell gently with the rhythm of the now-calm sea. *I must think of some way to get to shore,* she thought. *Just as soon as I've had a bit more rest....* Jocelyn allowed her eyes to close again.

"What should we do with it?" This was not the same voice as before, though it was no less haunting.

"Let us capsize its craft and be rid of the thing."

Jocelyn's eyes flew open. "Touch this boat," she said, "and you will find a bigger fight than you are bargaining for."

Laughter sang out again. The sisters ignored the girl, speaking only to one another.

"It appears that the ugly little beast is awake."

"Yes, and not in a very good mood, either."

"Didn't its mother teach it any manners?"

Jocelyn struggled to sit up, fighting waves of dizziness. "Why is it that those who are the most concerned with manners rarely have any themselves? How dare you hide out there in the dark, unwilling to show your faces, and yet carp on about my appearance?"

Her words had not yet stopped echoing over the waves when a long, thin creature shot out of the water. Though it was moving too fast for her to see it clearly, Jocelyn spied a flash of shiny scales and pale white skin. It arced over the boat, landing with a splash on the other side.

The girl leaned out, peering over the edge of the spare-spare. A woman's head and shoulders emerged from the water. Jocelyn's jaw dropped open. She was face-to-face with an actual mermaid.

I am not a poet (though I have been known to pen a limerick or two). As such, I have no words sufficient to describe the siren's splendor, nor that of her two sisters, surfacing to her either side. To say they were lovely is an insult. They were so much more. They were more exquisite than . . . let me think.

I've got it: more exquisite than a sturdy iron chest filled to the brim with gold doubloons, silver ducats, and all the crown jewels of Lithuania, and festooned with a red satin ribbon—but with a tag that says NOT FOR YOU.

Such was the mermaids' cruel beauty.

Jocelyn's fingers gripped the side of her boat as she studied the magnificent creatures. Under the light of the moon, their skin fairly glowed, flawless and dreadfully white. They reminded her of the dolls Sir Charles liked to get her from France. The girl smiled at the memory of those dolls: they were quite breakable.

Jocelyn needed help. As there was no one else about, she would have to get it from the mermaids. Appealing to their vanity appeared to be her best chance. "Please accept my most sincere apologies," she said. "I'm now certain that I was wrong. No one as breathtakingly beautiful as you could be considered ill-mannered."

Three pairs of perfect lips parted in haughty smiles.

She tried more flattery. "In addition to your, er, flawlessness"—she paused, trying to judge how her words were being received—"it is apparent that you are superior swimmers."

The mermaids moved closer to the girl's boat, some of their coldness seeming to thaw a bit under her contrite, and complimentary, attitude.

"It is true. We are superior to humans in every way."

"Oh yes," Jocelyn agreed, "utterly superior to humans, indeed. I consider myself lucky to have made your acquaintance."

"As you should, child. You are undeniably fortunate."

Jocelyn's fingers tightened on the edge of her boat. "Mmm-hmm, I really am. So, well, I don't quite know how to say this..."

Mermaids love only one thing more than their own reflections: praise. They can't get enough of it. "Go on, human. What is it you wish to say?"

"Could you—I mean to say—*would* you, please, push me to shore?" Jocelyn chose her words carefully, but they were still wrong.

Water churned around the creatures, tossing the dinghy to and fro. "How dare you?" The sisters roared like the waves. "We are not creatures to be placed in the servitude of humans! *We* are the superior beings; you should serve us."

The girl knew her situation was perilous. As such, she had nothing to lose. She pressed on. "If I don't get to shore, I could die—or worse. Please?"

"If you were not so hideous, we might consider doing something to help you. However, as there appears to be nothing about you worth saving, we would be completely justified in leaving you to your fate."

Now you have a correct idea of the nature of mermaids. They are terribly vain creatures, only concerned with beauty, chiefly their own. A particularly luscious pearl or an unusually intricate piece of coral would be given an appraising eye. A handsome sailor might attract some passing attention. But a desperate girl adrift at sea is nothing more than a pitiful curiosity. As Jocelyn seemed to be out of flattering words, the mermaids quickly lost interest.

Jocelyn wished she had something to throw at them. "Fine, don't help me, you slimy, smelly fish!" she shouted. "I hope you swim into a net and end up in a barrel of salted cod!"

Though she was not really in the mood to drown for the second time that day, Jocelyn almost hoped the mermaids would try to capsize her. She pulled her sword, itching to use it.

Mermaids never will do what you want them to. The sisters did not even dignify her outburst with a reply. In a motion so synchronized it could have been rehearsed (and most likely was), they pointed their perfect noses to the sky, turned their flawless backs, flipped their haughty tails, and dove beneath the water.

"Stupid mermaids!" Jocelyn called after them. Having done all she could to restore her pride, she sank down in the boat, struggling to remain hopeful that some other form of help would eventually arrive. She would just have to wait. Jocelyn tried to relax, but her growling stomach kept interrupting her. How long had it been since dinner?

"I wish I had a nice broiled fish," she said loudly, in case the mermaids were still listening.

The girl tried to resign herself to spending the night alone on Neverland waters in a dinghy without oars. The moon was bright enough to read by, if she had thought to bring a book along, but it hadn't crossed her mind during the whole pirates-trying-to-steal-her-ship-and-enslave-or-possibly-murder-the-crew affair. Jocelyn hoped her men were all right and that they were having a better time than she was, wherever they were.

Another few minutes passed. Jocelyn began to understand those unlucky sailors, stranded at sea without any wind to move them along, who sometimes go quite mad. Insanity would be far preferable to boredom. She squeezed her eyes shut and tried to muster up some lunacy, but to no avail. Having few other options, she decided that a song might help her pass the time:

> *It's all for me grog, me jolly, jolly grog,*
> *When I last went ashore for me furlough.*
> *There I spent all me dough on the lassies, don't you know,*
> *So across the Western Ocean I must wander....*

The song echoed over the water but quickly faded on Jocelyn's lips. Boisterous songs are best suited for a crowd, preferably one made up of scandalized old ladies, but out there, on her own in the dark... it was just too lonely.

Jocelyn wondered what Roger was doing with the lost boys, but quickly pushed that thought from her head. Instead she sighed and flipped open her locket for company, lay back in the bright moonlight, and gazed at her father's image. Without thought, she started to hum. Nothing specific, only a series of notes that felt in tune with the forlorn night. She opened her mouth and gave voice to the melody—softly at first, then louder—allowing the sound to soar up into the starry sky. The notes came rushing out as though a dam had broken, flooding the night. Every feeling held within Jocelyn's heart poured into the music. Heartbreak, loneliness, and sorrow paired off with resiliency, stubbornness, and wild hope. Pure emotion waltzed through her song, alive in the night.

Strong. Untamed. Breathtaking.

Jocelyn sang until there was nothing left, but instead of feeling empty, she felt filled. She drifted off to sleep, still tasting the song on her lips.

In her slumber, she missed seeing one of the rarest substances on earth: the tears of a mermaid.

CHAPTER TWENTY-NINE

Hunter and Hunted

Jocelyn was awakened, shortly after dawn, by a smell. In her case, it was rather pleasant, though I can attest that "pleasant" is not always a fitting label when one is woken by an odor.

Occasionally, my butler, Gregory, will eat rich foods too late in the evening, interrupting my slumber with the foulest of odors. And that is not Gregory's only fault. Just this morning, at breakfast, he wagged his tail at me, not once, but twice. Such impertinence, coupled with his nocturnal vapors, would be enough to get him sacked if I could find a suitable replacement. Unfortunately, no new applicant is willing to curl up in my lap on long winter evenings.

Jocelyn sensed the difference, even as she slept. Her boat no longer rocked on the waves. Warm sun kissed her bare arms. The cry of gulls tickled her sleeping ears. Best of all, a mouthwatering scent nuzzled her nose. She sat up and rubbed the last vestiges of sleep from her eyes.

The dinghy tilted to one side, aground on a rocky shore. Just up the beach, a cluster of mango trees beckoned. Behind her, in the sea, she heard a splash. Jocelyn turned just in time to see a flash of shiny scales. "Thank you," she whispered.

She climbed out of the boat and gingerly picked her way over the stones, regretting her lost shoe. When she reached the end of the rocks, Jocelyn sat down and pulled off the other. "I think no shoes are better than only one," she said, flinging it into a clump of sea grass. To make the deed complete, she balled up what was left of her stockings and tossed them away as well.

Eventually, and to the envy of all their friends and relations, a young chickadee couple would move into the shoe: *A silver-buckled brocade, on their income? How do they do it?*

Since she had no idea what to do next, Jocelyn lingered over a breakfast of juicy mangoes. "I wanted an adventure," she spoke aloud to herself, "and I got one, but not like I expected. If I ever make another wish, I'll try to remember to be more specific." She sat in silence, thinking a bit, before going on. "I can't do anything about

Roger. I can't get to my ship and help my crew. On my own, I don't know if I can defeat the crocodile." Remembering the way she had frozen in fear when she faced it, she thought, *I'm not even sure I can do it with help.*

Loud cawing interrupted her musings. A large black crow settled in the mango tree and picked at the fruit. Though it was not a creature she knew personally, she thought it likely he was a friend of Edgar's. They were both birds, after all.

This is much the way that all people from the same geographical area are sure to be familiar with one another: *Oh, you are from Lichtenstein? You must know Harold.*

"Excuse me," Jocelyn asked the bird, "do you know Edgar? He runs the courier service?"

The crow's beak was full of mango. Instead of speaking, it nodded.

Excellent. If Jocelyn could locate the courier, she could enlist his help in finding and rescuing her crew. Certainly he would have resources that could be of use. "Do you know where I can find him?"

The crow lifted a wing and pointed toward a thick stand of jungle growth. An overgrown path divided the trees.

"He lives down that way? About how far?"

It swallowed the bit of food in its mouth. "Not far," it replied, "as the crow flies."

"But I'm walking," Jocelyn said. The bird shrugged

and flew away. "Thank you for being so incredibly helpful!" she called after it, then muttered, "I hope he gets baked into a pie."

Finding Edgar somewhere up the path wasn't much of a plan, but it was better than nothing. She stood up, wiped mango juice from her mouth with the back of her hand, and started off.

Jocelyn hadn't gone more than a hundred yards into the jungle when she heard the ticking of a clock. The nightmare image of her father turning into the crocodile arose in her mind. Had the beast followed her here? In her dream, she had been unsure if the beast had been hunting her or if she had been hunting it. Even now she was uncertain, but she refused to wait for the monster to come and inform her.

She would not be pursued like a frightened rabbit. She pulled her sword from its sheath, left the path, and followed the dreadful ticktock.

Pushing aside a tangle of vines blocking her way, Jocelyn spied the beast, its massive snout snuffling at the ground as it lumbered through the underbrush. It was even more terrible on land. She could not seem to wrap her head around the size of the creature—easily twenty-five feet long. The crocodile's scarred, leathery hide was covered in dust, mud, and trailing bits of seaweed. Decay and despair hung about it like a noxious cloud.

I will not freeze. I will not freeze, Jocelyn repeated over and over in her head. In spite of herself, she retreated a step, snapping a twig underfoot.

The monster's head jerked up. It turned one appalling red eye on her, and terror erupted in her chest. She faltered, backing up another step. In a flash she was captured. Jocelyn dropped her sword as she was pulled right off her feet.

She had triggered some kind of trap; a net had sprang out of the dense jungle foliage and wrapped tightly around her. It pulled her up, snaring her high in a tree, a heartbeat before the crocodile burst through the undergrowth. She lay facedown, jumbled in a mass of thick ropes. The beast pushed back onto its hind legs and lunged for her. Jocelyn stared down into the creature's dark throat. A stench of rot and misery enveloped her.

The massive reptile stretched, higher and higher, straining to get to its prey, stopping mere inches from her face. It snapped and hissed in frustration, unable to reach. Relief coursed through the girl. She was safe.

But then, to her horror, she remembered that some crocodiles can jump. It recoiled back on its powerful haunches, preparing to spring.

From the thick jungle foliage, a volley of arrows flew toward the monster. They bounced off its thick hide, falling harmlessly in the underbrush. No damage was visible,

but the arrows did manage to distract it. The crocodile lowered itself to the ground, turning its head from side to side in an effort to locate the source of the arrows.

More arrows flew toward it. Again they bounced off its armor. The beast looked confused. It snapped its jaws in first one direction, then another. A third attack followed, then a fourth. Though no blood flowed, the archers finally succeeded in driving the monster away. It hissed at Jocelyn once more before lumbering off through the jungle.

Manly cheers erupted from the brush. However, if you were expecting Tiger Lily's braves to burst upon the scene, you are, unsurprisingly, wholly incorrect. The Neverland is home to a wide variety of native groups, tribes, clans, herds, and gaggles. Unlike pirates, lost boys, and girls playing at being mothers, the indigenous people do not come from anywhere. They merely spring up in the Neverland from time to time, as much a part of that clever island as her changeable mountain ranges and tidal flats.

The girl's rescuers, warriors from one such group of native Neverlandians, appeared, brandishing stone swords and finely crafted longbows. Jocelyn marveled. These men had not been afraid of the beast. Though her heart still pounded out a panicked rhythm, thoughts of the monster shrank at the sight of her saviors, gathered below. They could have stepped right out of the pages of an adventure book.

Eight mustachioed faces peered up at the girl in their snare. Their facial hair was impressive: brightly dyed and magnificently long (the most remarkable must have been at least an arm span from tip to tip). Jocelyn wondered how they managed to wax their whiskers into such stiff obedience. Sir Charles's mustache was much, much smaller, but it still drooped by midmorning.

Jocelyn was glad for the distraction. She preferred to focus on the men's faces, as they wore an embarrassing lack of clothing: nothing more than short trousers made of brightly colored cloth and feathers. Even their heads were uncovered, topped only by spiky hair in shades to match their fantastic whiskerature.

Though she tried not to focus on them, a quick peek at the men's shirtless torsos revealed a variety of fantastic tattoos, including one very familiar pattern. How bizarre it was that each of these Neverland warriors should sport the Union Jack, Great Britain's flag, across his upper back.

Two of the men untied the line securing their net and lowered Jocelyn to the ground. The rest of the group laughed and chattered in an unfamiliar language.

They are probably saying how glad they are that this trap saved me, although they must be sorry to have caught a girl instead of dinner, Jocelyn thought. Her face burned with shame. She would not have needed saving if she hadn't backed away from the crocodile. Perhaps if she had lunged, she might have bested it. In that case, instead of releasing her from the folds of the net, these strange men would be honoring her with a feast for freeing them from the tyranny of the monster.

Once she felt the solid ground again, Jocelyn stood to thank the circle of rescuers closing around her, even more fantastic and alien than they had first appeared. Closer inspection revealed their unusual face adornments to be not mustaches but large feathers sprouting from their nostrils. That explained the wonderful length and vivid hue. And what she had mistaken for hair was a patch of smaller feathers growing from the top of each of their heads. Their bright plumage, set against the seriousness of the men's faces, looked so comical that Jocelyn could not help but laugh. Several of the men lifted their swords in response.

"Please calm down," she said. "I did not mean to offend you. I'm only laughing because I've never seen anyone like you, either in the Neverland or in England."

The men smiled widely at her speech, mouths crowded with more teeth than seemed altogether decent. She heard a couple of them say, "Englee!"

"Yes, I see that you are familiar with my country. How did you happen to start wearing the Union Jack?"

The warriors made no reply to her question other than

to nudge one another, wink, and say, "Englee. Englee good."

Jocelyn tried speaking slower and louder so as to make herself understood.

"WHY—YOU"—she pointed at them—"HAVE—ENGLEE—FLAGEE"—she made a waving motion like a flag in the wind—"ON—YOUR—BACK?"

The men stopped smiling and exchanged glances. The kind of glances that seemed to say, *This person may be mad.* That must be a popular facial expression. I see it rather often.

One warrior reached out and pinched Jocelyn on the arm.

"Ouch! Stop that!" she said, slapping his hand away.

They roared with laughter, again saying, "Englee, good!"

In a very loud voice, the man with the longest feather mustache (bright yellow with sharply pointed ends) said, "WE—GO—TO—KARNAPINAE—VILLAGE"—he placed his fingertips together, forming a house shape—"AND—FEAST"—eating motions. "YOU—COME—QUICK—NOW. NO—TROUBLE—ENGLEE."

Satisfied that her way of communicating had proved effective, Jocelyn replied, "NO—NO—TROUBLE—AT—ALL!"

He nodded and, taking Jocelyn by the arm, led her down a nearby trail. Two warriors ran ahead, presumably to alert the village of their guest. The rest followed, each holding his sword at the ready.

Jocelyn hated that the men felt a need to protect her. To take her mind off her embarrassment, she asked the yellow-feathered man, "WHAT—ARE—WE—FEASTING—ON?"

Even though she spoke loudly and slowly, Yellow Feathers must not have understood, for he only nodded and said with a gleaming smile, "Englee!"

CHAPTER THIRTY

A Captive Audience with the King

Jocelyn and her new friends trekked through the jungle in silence, though the men continued to grin at her and mumble about "good Englee." Occasionally one or another reached out to pinch or poke at her. Though Jocelyn decided this must be a display of friendship, slapping their hands away was becoming wearisome.

Before long the scent of cooking fires and a small scattering of stone-and-thatch shelters signaled their arrival in the village. The Karnapinae women were absent, perhaps already preparing for the feast. A group of ragged children ran over to see the warriors' guest. They also had feathers growing from their heads and noses, though theirs were small and downy. Jocelyn wanted to ask the children more about their village, but they hung back shyly, staring.

Instead she grinned and waved, calling, "I'll see you at the feast!"

The children burst into wild laughter, as if she had said something particularly witty. Their easy merriment reminded Jocelyn of Roger. She wondered if he was, at that very moment, sharing a joke with the lost boys or, worse, Peter Pan. She dropped her hand and pulled her gaze away, her smile abandoning her face.

The group continued deeper into the village, finally stopping outside the largest dwelling. Odd stone pillars carved with teapots and English bulldogs flanked an open doorway. Tacked to the wall above it hung a tattered Union Jack. One of Jocelyn's escorts rudely prodded her backside with the blunt end of his spear and pointed to the dwelling. "YOU—SEE—KING. MAKE—READY—FOR—FEAST."

She scowled at him, rubbing at the sore spot. "There's no need to be rude. I wanted to see your old king anyway!" She marched through the entry, the men's laughter following her inside.

In the center of the hut sat a carved wooden throne, brightly painted and covered in precious stones. In contrast to the great chair, the wizened man upon it appeared quite frail and small.

He presented himself in dress and adornment much

like those Jocelyn was already acquainted with, although there were some subtle differences. While the warriors wore nothing on their heads, a covering of plaited reeds sat upon the old king's. It had a rounded top and a slightly turned-up brim running all the way around.

The king's clothing, or rather, his lack of, looked no different from anyone else's. It revealed a wrinkled body covered with distorted tattoos. Jocelyn longed for him to turn around. This would give her the opportunity to see if he sported the same design as his warriors on his upper back—and also keep her from having to look at his shriveled chest and belly.

Nasal feathers of the deepest vermilion sprouted from his nostrils. They were longer than any the girl had yet seen and quivered with every breath. While Jocelyn studied the king's nose feathers, he took a deep breath, causing them to bob emphatically. "Are you afflicted with either hearing loss or some sort of mental incapacity?"

Jocelyn eyes widened. "You speak perfect English."

"Of course. All Karnapinaes learn to speak English at a young age, though none command the language quite as well as I. One of my messengers, when he informed me you were coming to our village, said you had an infirmity of either the ears or the mind. It appears he was mistaken."

Jocelyn's cheeks flushed, but she replied, "Hmmm, did he now? I wonder what gave him that impression."

Eager to change the subject, she asked about the king's unusual hat.

"This is modeled on a very popular English style, the bowler," he answered proudly. "Do you not recognize it? Perhaps it is from a different When than you have come from."

"Perhaps it is," Jocelyn agreed. "I can't imagine my grandfather choosing to wear that style, but somehow it suits you. You seem to be quite well versed in English language and fashions. How did that come about, here in the Neverland? Do you have many English visitors?" Jocelyn asked.

"Not nearly as many as we would like," he replied. "I will tell you a bit of the history of the Karnapinae so that you may understand our great interest in your country." The king straightened on his throne, obviously pleased to share his story. "We learned of your great land from my father. He was the first of our people to discover how to fly with his nose feathers.

"At the time, he was a young man, not yet ready to take on the responsibilities of leadership. His journeys took him all over this world and into the other. After many seasons, he found the land your people call England. Though my father wished never to leave that place, his duty was here. He returned home to lead our people, but he never forgot. Of all the places on earth, he found England to be the most delicious."

That's an odd way to describe it, Jocelyn thought.

"No one has made the long journey since. My father died while I was yet young, and I became king of the Karnapinae people. My responsibilities have kept me here. Being unable to taste such wonders myself, I jealously ordered my people not to attempt the flight. Now I am old and can no longer travel the great distances that are required. I dream of sending my sons in my place as soon as their nose feathers grow large enough to carry them.

"It is my desire that they may fit unobtrusively into society, to keep from alarming the livestock—rather, the English citizens. Thus I have educated them, and all my people, in the ways of yours. Now you are here, and you can add to their knowledge. You have little time to teach my people all you know before we have you at our afternoon feast."

"I can do that," Jocelyn agreed, "but with two conditions. First, please tell me, why were your men unafraid of the crocodile? Everyone else seems to be terrified in its presence."

"That is simple. My warriors do feel dread at the sight of the beast, but they push it aside when they must. In this case they wanted you more than they feared the monster."

Jocelyn flushed. "How kind of them. I must remember to say thank you. My second condition is this: I need to return to my ship. My crew is in trouble, and I have to help them. Could you send some of your warriors to accompany me after the feast?"

The old king frowned. "This I cannot do. Perhaps you do not understand. You will not be a guest at the feast. Instead, you will have the great honor of becoming the main dish."

With a snap of his fingers, the king summoned Yellow Feathers into the hut. The warrior clamped the struggling girl between his strong hands, holding her still while the king gave instructions. Yellow Feathers would accompany Jocelyn to the feast preparation site, where the rest of the kingdom was assembling. There the girl would be privileged to nourish first the Karnapinaes' minds—and then their bodies.

With a wink, the king tipped his homemade bowler hat, and Jocelyn was dragged from the hut.

CHAPTER THIRTY-ONE

Teaching Table Manners to Cannibals

There's an old saying: "Time flies when you are about to be peeled and boiled." On second thought, perhaps it goes, "Being peeled and boiled attracts flies, in time." Or it may be about thyme... quite a nice herb, it is. Old sayings are not really my forte.

At any rate, it would not be long until the feast. Jocelyn needed to find a way to avoid becoming the main course.

She kicked and fought, but her captor paid no attention. She frantically tried to sort out some kind of escape plan, but panic had muddled her thinking. Since Jocelyn had dropped her sword when she triggered the snare, she didn't even have a weapon.

All too soon they arrived at the heart of the village. Clearly, the cannibals were anticipating a grand party.

Bright ribbons and more feathers festooned the few trees and shrubs growing nearby. A cooking pot, big as a bathtub, bubbled merrily on the fire. It was surrounded by long tables, also brightly adorned. There was ample seating for the village's entire adult population.

The children were not invited, having been forced into partaking of that barbaric custom known the world over as nap time. Jocelyn had been well acquainted with this practice herself through her childhood series of nurses and governesses. Adults often claim naps to be healthful, for growing children need their rest, but the fact of the matter is, grown-ups find pursuing their own interests much more enjoyable without the little dears constantly underfoot.

Groups of Karnapinae women, freed from the tyranny of their offspring, laughed and gossiped while they chopped vegetables. A sickening feeling formed in Jocelyn's stomach as she realized they were preparing her side dishes. Again she struggled against her captor, but Yellow Feathers shoved Jocelyn to the ground, threatening her with the point of his stone sword. She stood and dusted herself off, tasting blood in her mouth. She had bitten her cheek.

At least I got the first bite.

Jocelyn felt hysterical laughter rise in her throat. With a sharp prod to her arm, the warrior cut off her giggles before they were fully born. Though the wound was little more than a scratch, it did serve to clear her head.

*If the great Captain Hook were surrounded by hungry can-
nibals bent on having Pirate Stew for dinner, what would
he do?*

He'd likely stab his hook into every last one of them.

Unfortunately, that wouldn't work for Jocelyn. She
needed another plan.

Yellow Feathers called the villagers to attention. They
gathered around, standing to face the girl, each anxious to learn more about the "Englee." When she did
not begin speaking right away, Jocelyn received a second
prod from the warrior's sword. A drop of blood welled up
where he had poked her. Several in the audience licked
their lips.

She clapped her hand over the tiny cut, hiding it
from view. "Someone needs to teach you people some
manners!"

Jocelyn imagined Miss Eliza here with this group of
half-naked Neverlandians, forcing them to sit through
one of her lectures on the proper way to hold a soupspoon. The absurd thought threatened to bring back
Jocelyn's laughter, but before it could bubble out, she had
the most marvelous idea.

She choked back her nervousness and began, "Hello,
barbaric cannibals. Your king has asked me to give you
some instruction on English society before the feast
begins. This seems a perfect time to teach you proper
table manners." Jocelyn paused, collecting her thoughts.

Using her best impression of Miss Eliza's instruction-time voice she went on. "In order to blend into high society, you must never eat without remembering, and exhibiting, *all* the rules of etiquette. To breach these rules is to bring shame and dishonor upon your entire family."

As a group, the cannibals stood up straighter, eyes wide. Jocelyn continued: "Each gentleman will offer his left arm to a lady. Ladies, gently grasp his arm directly below the elbow with your right hand. Allow him to escort you to the table."

The Karnapinaes eagerly followed her instructions and looked to her for more.

"Gentlemen, bow to the lady. Ladies, curtsy in return. Lower. Loooower."

A few of the women curtsied so deeply they were unable to get back up without assistance. Jocelyn glared at them. "If you are quite finished making fools of yourselves, we will continue. Now, ladies, allow the gentlemen to help you with your chair. Gentlemen, remain standing until the last lady has been seated. Never place your elbows on the table. Sit up straight. Do not fidget; do not kick. Gentlemen, remove your weapons and place them under your chairs."

They did it. Every last one of the warriors put his weapon under his chair and looked to his instructor for praise. She did not offer any.

It was thrilling to wield the power of a manners mistress.

"Do not breathe loudly or make other bodily noises at the table. Do not pick your teeth. Ever." She paused to think. What else did Miss Eliza say? Jocelyn wished now that she had paid more attention to her lessons, but how was she to know that a working knowledge of etiquette might one day prove useful in saving her from becoming Cannibal Cassoulet?

The Karnapinaes misinterpreted the girl's silence as the end of their lesson and broke into applause. One cannibal, a middle-aged woman said, "Thank you for sharing Englee wisdom. We now prepare the meat!"

The meat was not at all prepared to be prepared. "Oh, no," Jocelyn quickly went on, "we are only getting started. There are many, many more rules to remember. You must learn them if you are to fit into English society one day. If you don't, you'll never be granted an audience with the King of England."

The Karnapinaes gave a collective gasp, staring at the girl in obvious horror. The woman bowed her head. "Forgive me, Englee. I very much want to eat Englee royalty."

"Who wouldn't?" Jocelyn replied, continuing with her lesson. "Wait until your host or hostess unfolds his or her table linen before lifting yours, using your *right* hand only. Never use the left. That would be shameful. Unfold the napkin and gently place it in your lap."

The cannibals were lost in bewilderment. Their king had not yet arrived. In his absence they were unsure as to who the host or hostess might be.

The girl smiled a wicked smile at their discomfort. "The first course is soup. Do not begin eating until your host or hostess has taken his or her first bite. Use your soupspoon only. Never use a salt spoon, teaspoon, compote spoon, grapefruit spoon"—Jocelyn took a deep breath and went on—"demitasse spoon, caviar spoon, egg spoon, or runcible spoon—"

Yellow Feathers boldly interrupted. "Karnapinae people have one spoon only, Englee girl."

"Then use your imagination," Jocelyn snapped. "Just be sure to imagine the correct utensil." She cleared her throat. "As I was saying, a soupspoon, and only a soupspoon, is acceptable for soup. Remember this rhyme: 'As all the ships go out to sea, I spoon my soup *away* from me.' Sip your soup quietly. No matter how hot, never, ever blow on it.

"The second course is—"

She was interrupted by a weary young woman asking, "How many courses, Englee?"

Jocelyn glared until the woman looked away, ashamed. The girl was beginning to enjoy herself. "There are generally twelve courses"—the dining party groaned, but Jocelyn pretended not to notice—"though on formal occasions there may be up to twenty-nine, each with its own set of rules and cutlery. I hope you are all paying close attention so as not to embarrass yourselves tonight at the feast."

Learning they would have to use their new knowledge that very evening alarmed the Karnapinaes. Each sat up even straighter and looked as though he or she was trying very hard to pay attention.

Jocelyn showed no mercy. "As I was saying, the second course is fish. You will use your fish fork. Not your crab fork, berry fork, pudding fork, meat fork, pickle fork..."

The cannibal king arrived in the middle of Jocelyn's instruction on the eighth course (Roasted Rutabaga Ragout). Not wanting him to miss out, Jocelyn began again, from the start. By the time she finished with the rules for course twelve (Jellied Egg Custard), everyone was too terrified to eat.

At that point escape was easy. Jocelyn told her audience to practice a bit while she observed. No one even noticed her slip away. All eyes were glued to the table, surely imagining the horror of using the wrong piece of cutlery. Jocelyn crept off, leaving the people to their sad fate.

I am told the entire party stared at their plates, unmoving, until they starved to death. No one wanted to commit the terrible faux pas of using an asparagus fork when an ice cream fork was called for.

The Karnapinae children grew up wild, utterly rebelling against the customs of their parents. They left the village and became vegetarians, subsisting entirely on a diet of greens and coffee, which they would consume while stroking their feathery mustaches and discussing philosophy.

From what I understand, even now, if you happen to stumble upon the ruined remains of their old village, you can still see the elder cannibals' skeletons gathered round the table, resplendent nose feathers rippling in the breeze.

It's a pity that they are gone. I would have loved to have had the original Karnapinae people round for dinner with my lawyer.

CHAPTER THIRTY-TWO

In Which Jocelyn Kills the Reptile

Jocelyn's spirits were high after her encounter
with the Karnapinaes. She may have been nothing more than a young, unarmed girl, but she had
matched wits with an entire small kingdom of bloodthirsty cannibals and won. Even better, she had done it
in her own way.

How surprising to find that Jocelyn's education at Miss
Eliza Crumb-Biddlecomb's Finishing School for Young
Ladies had actually come in useful. Think on that next
time you are bemoaning your mathematics homework.

Jocelyn considered her original plan of locating Edgar,
trusting that he would be able to secure some kind of help
in rescuing her crew. She only hoped she could find her
men before the crocodile found her. Though she wasn't

ready to give up on her quest to avenge her father, she did not want to face the monster on her own again. It was ever so much worse than cannibals.

She reached for the compass in her pocket before remembering that it was gone. If only Roger hadn't chosen to forget her—they could rescue her crew and fight the beast together. But thinking about Roger wasn't going to solve her problems. She resolved to put him out of her mind and figure out what to do next.

First, Jocelyn wanted her sword. Then she'd go looking for Edgar and find a way to save her men from Captain Krueger. Just thinking about what that horrible man might be doing with her crew made the girl's head ache with worry—though she knew that fretting wouldn't solve anything. She squared her shoulders and marched up the trail.

The way back felt longer than she remembered. Hours passed, marked by the constant rumbling of her stomach. This time the island did not offer her mangoes, or anything else. The shade deepened, and even in a tropical jungle the cool snap of autumn hung in the air. The prospect of spending the night alone and unarmed was a bit worrisome.

Finally, Jocelyn returned to the area where she had been captured. In their excitement at taking her prisoner, the Karnapinae warriors had neglected to reset their snare. The net lay in a crumpled heap, clearly marking the spot. To her great relief, she spied a glint of silver in the brush. She picked up her sword, polished it on the ragged hem of her dress, and returned it to its sheath.

A movement in the foliage caught Jocelyn's eye. For a moment she was unable to puzzle out what had caused it. All that registered was an enormous mass of scales and serpentine muscle.

To refer to the creature as a snake would be a gross understatement. Yet "uncommonly large cylindrical reptile" is such a mouthful, wouldn't you agree? For the purpose of ease in speaking, I'll use the more convenient term, but you must promise not to underestimate.

The snake's length proved impossible to guess, as it lay coiled in a twisting, writhing pile; its girth, however, was easily that of Jocelyn's leg. It was a murky gray, nearly black, with a sickly green underbelly. If it hadn't been for that dark coloring, the girl might not have noticed the miniature victim trapped in the snake's grip. A faint glow shone from a tiny humanlike leg wedged between its clenched coils. Jocelyn gasped.

The only real fairy she had met thus far had not left a good impression. Still, the girl had read enough to be relatively well-informed as to their general character. Sometimes the wee folk were pleasant and good to humans, but usually not. More often they liked to play pranks and wreak havoc. As such, Jocelyn felt that they were kindred spirits. She simply could not let one be killed by a snake.

"Listen to me, you vile beast. I command you to release that poor creature at once."

The viper bared its fangs and hissed, continuing to squeeze its prey. The fairy's light was growing dimmer. It did not appear to have much time left. Jocelyn picked up a stick and whacked the reptile across the back. It bounced off with a thud.

"I said, put it down!"

Slowly, but without releasing its captive, the snake stretched toward the girl. Her heart pounded in her chest, but she stood her ground. Coil by coil, it unwound. Jocelyn heard the crackling of fallen leaves as the snake's heavy body crushed them to powder. A musky odor hung in the air as it pulled back and prepared to strike.

Joceyln blinked, and the serpent's head was flying through the air, mouth open, razor-sharp fangs coming straight for her face. Jocelyn struck without thinking. She felt the familiar grip of the sword in her hand and wondered how it had gotten there. At her feet lay the headless snake, its cold red blood soaking into the ground.

She stared at the carnage for a few seconds before remembering the fairy. It took her some time to find the tiny being, buried as it was in the still-twitching remains. When at last she located it, the fairy was not moving.

Jocelyn cradled the little creature in her palm, peering closely. It was male, and if her fairy tales had been correct, his faint blue coloring indicated him to be noble—possibly even royal. Things did not look promising. His body was crushed into an unnatural shape, with one fragile wing slightly torn. Worse yet, he lay absolutely still, not appearing to breathe. Even in the deep jungle shade, the fairy's light was so faint Jocelyn could hardly see it.

Killing the snake had not saved him. Her efforts had made no difference.

The fairy would die.

CHAPTER THIRTY-THREE

*Never Discount Advice
Learned in Fairy Tales*

It has been my experience that mortal wounds, in
oneself or another, can occasionally put a damper
on an otherwise good day. Jocelyn didn't even have
the heart to exult in her victory over the snake. It was
completely overshadowed by the dying fairy cradled in
her hands.

She held the broken creature close to her face, searching for signs of life, but it lay cold and dark in her palm.
Jocelyn had seen death before—in the occasional bird
or small animal in the gardens surrounding her grandfather's home. And when the oldest and gentlest of Sir
Charles's hunting dogs had become sick and died, she'd
cried at its loss. But nothing the girl had ever experienced

was as cruel and shocking as the lifelessness of that tiny fairy. The very wrongness of it was obscene.

Jocelyn sank to her knees. Twigs and rocks bit into her, but she didn't care. She was intent only on the little man. "No!" she cried. "No! You can't die. I didn't fail this time. I defeated the snake. Please don't die!"

She stared intently at the fairy, as though her attention could stop death from completing its task.

"You can pull through. I know you can. Please. I believe in you. . . ."

Perhaps it was only her imagination, but Jocelyn thought she felt him stir. "Are you still with me?" she whispered. "You are, aren't you? Please wake up. I believe in you."

The weak trill of a bell—a moan—escaped his tiny lips. Jocelyn felt positively giddy with relief. "You're not dead!"

Light blossomed like a tiny sunrise in her hand. The fairy shook his head, ever so slightly.

"I knew it!" she exclaimed. "Thank goodness! Are you badly hurt?"

He opened one eye, peeked at her, and vigorously nodded.

"Oh, dear," Jocelyn said. "What can I do to help?"

The fairy merely shrugged.

"Can I take you to your home?"

Another shrug accompanied with a yawn.

"Can I get you something for the pain?"

This time he grinned and nodded again.

"What is it? I'll get it for you," she asked with an eager smile.

He spoke, but Jocelyn could not understand. She only heard the tinkling of bells.

"I'm sorry, I don't know what you mean," she said. "Could you point it out?"

He pointed at her.

"Yes, I'll help you. I only need to know what you want."

The fairy shot up out of her hand and kissed the corner of her lips. His light erupted into a brilliant glow as he settled back into her still-outstretched hand.

Flustered, she stammered, "Oh, um, that..."

Though the little man was obviously feeling much better, his torn wing made it impossible for him to fly well. Jocelyn placed him on her shoulder and conducted him where he wished to go. He gave directions by pointing and pulling at her hair in an affectionate manner.

The jungle foliage soon gave way to a woodland forest filled with a soft tinkling sound. They were getting close. Peering through the fragrant pines at the edge of a clearing, Jocelyn beheld the most astonishing sight of her young life.

Hundreds of tiny fairies lit up the darkening sky. They flitted about singly and in pairs, dancing to the merry music of a frog orchestra. Mushroom-cap tables were laden with fine acorn platters piled high with tiny, savory-smelling delicacies. Jocelyn's stomach lodged another complaint with the management regarding the length of time since breakfast.

At the edge of the clearing sat the fairy queen herself. Attendants and courtiers flanked Her Majesty's delicate lily throne, each appearing desperate for her favor. The queen wore a gown of fine spider silk—white, of course. Members of the royal family are the only fairies allowed to wear pure white. It perfectly contrasts with the blue blood glowing through their translucent skin.

I rarely wear white myself. Bloodstains are too difficult to remove.

Jocelyn had never seen anything lovelier than the miniature queen. She could not tear her eyes away. The little man on her shoulder had to pinch her ear in order to regain the girl's attention. Jocelyn looked up in time to see more fairies, soldiers dressed in red leaf jackets, flying in formation. They advanced upon the girl, holly-leaf lancets pointed directly at her face. The fairy man shot crookedly up from her shoulder, bells ringing furiously. The soldiers halted in midair and bowed.

Jocelyn glanced back at the queen. Their eyes met. Thankfully, the girl remembered her manners and exhibited a curtsy so deep that even Miss Eliza would have been impressed. The fairy queen nodded her favor, beckoning Jocelyn forward. The diminutive sovereign clapped her hands three times and her golden lily grew, rising upon its delicate stem until the ruler and girl were eye to eye.

Jocelyn determined not to blink at the queen's searching stare. Her Majesty's black eyes, no larger than the head of a pin, appeared to hold the answers to all of life's mysteries: *Who are we? Why are we here? What is the meaning of life? Why isn't cake considered a breakfast food?* After what seemed a very long time, the fairy looked away. Jocelyn sighed with relief. She had begun to feel restless.

The queen pulled a delicate silver bell from within the folds of her robes and rang it. Echoes of its sweet peals hung on the air, but instead of dying out, the sound grew stronger. The orchestra stopped playing. Jocelyn expected the dancing to cease as well, but a new dance began with the bell's one-note song growing louder in the air.

The fairies arranged themselves into a ring and performed a series of complicated steps. In the center of the circle, soft earth bulged upward until it split open. A trickle of water burbled out. The dancers' speed increased and the spray grew larger, fountaining into the air. The fairies now moved so fast that they seemed a blur. Jocelyn heard a loud crack like the sound of walking on the frozen surface of a late-winter pond.

The bell's sound died out. The dancers stood still. The fountain had vanished. In its place stood a delicate crystal goblet, large enough for a human to use, filled to the brim with a rich amber liquid. Three large fairies with dragonfly wings carefully lifted it, flew over, and placed it on the ground in front of Jocelyn.

The queen nodded again and motioned toward the drink. Gingerly, the girl picked it up. She wondered if she should drink. Many fairy tales spoke about those who foolishly consumed fairy food or drink and became trapped, prisoners forever in the queen's realm.

Jocelyn had always scoffed at such nonsense. If everyone who drank became captive, who would be left to tell the stories? Still, it was one thing to laugh away a tale safely ensconced between the pages of a book. It was quite another thing to consider such information while holding a goblet of fairy ambrosia in the middle of an enchanted wood.

Jocelyn lifted the cup to her nose and inhaled. It smelled like an August night, ripe and sweet. Moonlight glinted off the glass, causing the liquid inside to sparkle. She suddenly felt very thirsty. Perhaps one tiny sip wouldn't hurt. Just enough to moisten her lips.

As soon as she brought the goblet to her mouth, Jocelyn's thirst took over. She drank deeply until the glass, now empty, slipped from her fingers and smashed on the ground below.

The girl barely had time to think, *What have I done?* before the earth tilted sharply. A thousand points of light danced before her eyes. She feebly reached out to swat at them, but they were too quick for her. Her hand felt nothing but empty air. They swirled about, making her dizzy. She closed her eyes and tried to concentrate.

Jocelyn breathed in and tasted the cool night air. It carried away some of the overpowering sweetness that the drink had left on her tongue. As her head cleared, the girl realized that she was lying on the ground, cool dew soaking into her dress.

Jocelyn cracked open her eyes and saw that the swirling lights had only been the starry night sky, thankfully now still, staring down at her. The North Star gave an impertinent wink.

"Are you quite well, child? I do apologize for being unable to prepare you for the effects of fairy nectar. I understand that this can be rather startling for humans."

Jocelyn turned her head to the source of the voice. It was the fairy queen who had spoken, but something was off about her. She was too close, too large. It looked as if Jocelyn were viewing her from the wrong end of her spyglass.

"Meriwether, perhaps you could assist the girl?"

Warm hands gently pulled Jocelyn to her feet. She swayed, leaning in to the one who had aided her. It was a boy who didn't appear to be much older than Jocelyn, though he was rather taller. She had to tilt her head to see his face. His features were surprising. It was not his deep black eyes, his long, straight nose, nor his laughing mouth. No, what surprised Jocelyn most was his faintly glowing skin.

It was blue.

If Jocelyn had been the kind of girl who was prone to fainting, the sight of a pair of wings, one somewhat crumpled, growing out of the boy's back would have surely been cause for the smelling salts. As it was, Jocelyn merely sat back down on the ground and stared.

He bowed. "Thank you for saving me. I am in your debt."

The boy was the fairy she had rescued.

Jocelyn had been changed, reduced down to the size of the fairies. The girl's folly crashed over her.

She had drunk their nectar and could never go back.

CHAPTER THIRTY-FOUR

Choices

"**M**y son is quite taken with you, child."

Jocelyn sat upon a soft chair in Queen Mab's private chambers, high in an old oak tree. The queen felt that a bit of solitude might help Jocelyn overcome the disorienting effects of such a drastic size change. Therefore Her Majesty had commanded that only twelve fairies-in-waiting attend to her and the girl.

Attend they did. They washed and rinsed Jocelyn's tangled curls and scrubbed the dirt from her face and hands. Jocelyn didn't exactly enjoy the attention, but she had far greater problems to worry about—and at least they were gentler maidservants than Gerta. She didn't even resist (much) when they dressed her in a new gown.

Thankfully, fairies had no use for corsets, or there would have been a good sight more difficulty.

"There, now. Look at yourself, my dear. You are absolutely stunning," Queen Mab said, handing her a dewdrop mirror. The fairies had done their work well, but Jocelyn much preferred the way she had looked that afternoon: hair wild and dirt on her face, dress stained and wrinkled with one of its buttons broken, another missing, and a bit of flowering weed tucked in the otherwise unoccupied buttonhole.

Though her reflection didn't show it, Jocelyn still felt a bit disoriented. She only half listened as the queen continued: "My son has always been attracted to adventure, and you practically exude it through your very pores. Something tells me you two could be quite a pair. That is, of course, should you select to stay with us."

Jocelyn's head cleared. She waved off a fairy-in-waiting who was trying to smooth her rough nails. "Are you saying that if I want to I can return to my normal size and leave?"

"Of course, child. Did you think we would bestow the gift of immortality upon you without your consent?"

"I had read stories—"

"Silly fairy tales, no doubt. At sunrise, should you desire to accept our gift and dwell here forever, you will sprout wings and become my ward, a fairy princess. If you choose to return to the human world, I will grant you another wish in its stead, to express my gratitude for Meriwether's life. At dawn you will tell me your choice." The queen gave a regal yawn. "I grow weary of this discussion; let us return to the ball."

A young fruit bat carried Jocelyn down from the tree. The prince stepped up to greet her and bowed a second time. "We haven't been formally introduced. I am Meriwether Pennyroyal. Thank you again for saving my life."

"Oh. Well. Thank you for not dying."

He dropped his formal demeanor and asked eagerly, "Have you decided to stay?"

"I'm not sure, though I am glad to have a choice. I don't like to be forced to do things."

"If you do, you will be a princess—that means no one could make you do anything you don't like. Think how much fun we could have."

Jocelyn had to admit the thought was tempting. She looked over at the fairies dancing in the moonlight and imagined herself as one of them. What would her wings look like? A butterfly? A dragonfly? Hopefully not like that dreadful man standing off to the side with his cockroach wings folded about him.

She tried to picture herself flying along beside the fairy boy and having adventures, but couldn't get the image right. In her head, Meriwether had curly hair and brown skin instead of blue.

"Do you dance?" Meriwether asked, sounding very much like the someone else she had been thinking of. She pushed the memory from her head and allowed the prince to escort her to the circle of dancers. His hand was warm and dry, unlike those of the sweaty boys Jocelyn had been forced to pair with at Miss Eliza's Christmas ball. To her surprise, she did not find dancing with the fairy at all unpleasant. Meriwether led Jocelyn through the steps, and she matched them, feeling like quite a different sort of person than she was before.

After some time, the prince released her hand and tapped her necklace. "What is this talisman you are wearing?"

"Oh, that. It's a locket." She opened it to reveal the portrait of her father.

Her father.

If she stayed with the fairies, she'd no longer have to worry about his request and the crocodile. The thought filled her with relief, disappointment, and an unexpected twinge of sadness. Jocelyn did want to succeed, but it was so much harder than she'd imagined it would be.

And what about her crew? No matter what she chose, she couldn't just abandon them. If she decided to remain human, she could wish for the kind of strength that would enable her to both save them and defeat the crocodile. That would surely make her the greatest pirate ever to live—no one would doubt that.

But was becoming the world's greatest pirate what she really wanted? Or was it only another way of dancing to someone else's music?

If she were a fairy princess, couldn't she find a way to free her crew anyway? After that she could forget all about the crocodile and just do fairy things, whatever they might be.

Lost as Jocelyn had been in her thoughts and the ball, she did not notice the sky steadily growing lighter. When she saw the faint gray of predawn, she panicked. The sun would be up any moment, but she didn't know what she wanted. To become a fairy princess or to avenge her father?

The first rays of the sun peeked over the horizon. Queen Mab stood before her, compelling her to make her choice.

But which one? Pirate or princess?

Meriwether looked imploringly at her.

Princess or pirate?

Jocelyn didn't know who to be. She wanted someone to help her sort it out, but there was no time left.

"You must decide, my child. What do you desire?"

"I—"

What did she want?

"I want my mother!"

The earth tilted again. Jocelyn sank into oblivion.

CHAPTER THIRTY-FIVE

The Killer of Fairies and Childhood Dreams

Jocelyn rubbed her eyes, taking in the green forest around her. She sat with her back to a tree, nestled in soft ferns. Filtered rays of the sun paraded up and down on the girl's comfortably ruined dress. She touched the wilted flower in her buttonhole.

What am I doing here?

Waking in an unfamiliar place can be rather disorienting, or so I've been told. It can also be quite entertaining—if you do not happen to be the one experiencing it. My old aunt Sophia was afflicted with bouts of narcolepsy: falling asleep without warning and at the most inopportune times. One minute she'd be chatting away about dress fashions or gunpowder prices; the next she was slumped over, unconscious.

My cousins and I made a bit of sport with the old lady. She would wake to find herself picnicking in a field of flowers, propped up at the tea table entertaining the vicar and his wife, or tucked into a long box, buried six feet under the ground, with only a coffin bell for her amusement—any number of delightful situations. She always had a good laugh, once she finished weeping.

Being of sterner stuff than my aunt Sophia, Jocelyn did not cry out in tearful horror, but she did blink her eyes and wonder. Like a half-forgotten dream, images from the night before surfaced in her mind: the fairy nectar, the dancing . . . her wish.

She looked around in hopeful anticipation, but Jocelyn was utterly alone.

Stupid fairies, she thought as she stood and kicked the gnarled tree trunk she had rested against. *Didn't I know better than to trust a wish?*

The girl got to her feet, looking for some landmark to tell her which way to go. Standing alone in the stillness of the forest, she got a strange feeling. Something was different. There was a scent in the air, familiar to the child but foreign to the Neverland. She closed her eyes and breathed in, trying to remember where she knew it from.

When she opened her eyes, Jocelyn found herself somewhere else entirely. The forest had gone, replaced by a bedroom suite dressed in weathered gold-and-ivory wallpaper. Rich, dark furnishings adorned the space, conveying warmth, wealth, and yet a feeling distinctly feminine. Jocelyn found herself seated upon a stool facing a beautifully carved dressing table. A copy of *Gulliver's Travels* lay at the table's edge. She spied her own eyes in the large mirror before her. They were wide, unbelieving, for she knew this room: it had been her mother's.

Sir Charles had expressly forbidden Jocelyn from entering Evelina's old room, so naturally it had become her favorite childhood play place. Oh, how she had loved looking at and trying on the jewels found in the dressing table's right-hand drawer, imagining them to be stolen treasure. (Of course, as they were gifts to her mother from her father, she was likely correct about that.) She opened the drawer and was delighted to find all her favorites still there. Her fingertips lingered over their glimmering surfaces, though she did not try them on. Instead she turned her attention to the items cluttering the top of the table. In addition to the book, she spied her mother's heavy silver hairbrush and combs, a billowy powder puff, and several dainty bottles filled with expensive perfumes. Under the girl's touch each item felt heavy, burdened with stories Jocelyn would never be a part of.

She lifted her favorite bottle, stirring up the dust lying thick upon the cut crystal. Undoing its stopper, Jocelyn recognized the scent she had been unable to place in the forest. She glanced at the mirror and beheld an image of her much younger self trying on the perfume. She watched herself, remembering. She had thought of her mother as she played with her things—wondering what it would be like if Evelina had lived, wondering why she had died, leaving her child behind.

The memory surrounded her, poking at the empty place in her heart. Jocelyn's eyes stung. She gripped the bottle tightly, the pattern on the crystal biting into her hand. The young girl in the mirror looked up, her eyes shining. She slowly vanished, changing into a reflection of Jocelyn's current self—older, but still alone.

It was so unfair!

Jocelyn hurled the perfume bottle with all her might, smashing both it and the mirror into a thousand shards. She threw another, and another. In a matter of moments the tabletop was transformed, its once beautiful bottles reduced to shattered glass and pooling liquid. She held the last unbroken one in her fist, her energy drained away. The scent rising from the ruin was too sweet, too strong, and it burned the girl's throat. Tears threatened, but Jocelyn refused to give in. Instead she let out an angry, frustrated scream. "Why did you leave me behind?" she cried. "I would have gone with you! Why did you leave me alone?" It is a sad fact that the child, though thinking of her mother, could have been addressing either parent.

A cool hand on her shoulder startled the girl. She turned and saw the calm face of a lovely lady. Something about the curve of her cheek and the slight upturn of her nose echoed Jocelyn's own features. "Mother?" the girl whispered. There was no one else it could have been.

The woman smiled softly down. "Could this be my baby, grown so big at last?"

Things rarely come to pass in the way you imagine them. Jocelyn had often dreamed about what it might be like to meet her mother. Now, given the opportunity, she did not feel at all how she'd thought she would.

"If you hadn't died, you would know who I am." She frowned. "You wouldn't have to ask."

"Oh, Jocelyn," her mother said. "Please know that I didn't want to leave. It was simply my time."

"I don't care. You have no idea what it was like growing up with only my grandfather—knowing that no matter what I did, I'd never be as perfect or lovely as you were." Jocelyn squeezed the bottle in her hand, tempted to hurl it as she had the rest.

"I understand quite a lot more than you think. Remember, your grandfather is my father. I learned to look forward to my own future with nothing more than polite boredom. Without consulting me, he bought a ridiculous ship and sent me out for a pleasure cruise, in order to attract 'the right sort' of attention. The only attention it attracted was your father's. When I saw James for the first time, I knew my future would be something quite different from what my father had planned. I could choose for myself."

"But you left him, too. That's what you do. You leave."

"With your father, life was an adventure, but he was not a benevolent man. He committed many terrible acts in his life—so many, in fact, that wickedness poisoned his very blood. As much as I loved him, it was not easy to live each day under his dark shadow. I didn't want to leave, but in the end we both agreed it was best."

"If my father was so wicked, how could you have loved him in the first place? You were so perfect."

Evelina laughed. "No one is perfect, Jocelyn—certainly not I. In the same way, no one is perfectly terrible, though James would have liked to think that he came close. He had deep feelings: love, loneliness, passion—"

"Disgusting."

"—but he kept his humanity, truly everything dear to him, locked up tight in an iron box. A box to which, I'm afraid, he refused to share the key."

A memory itched at the back of Jocelyn's mind, but she couldn't quite scratch it.

"When I returned home and learned I would be your mother, it was the happiest time of my life. The last thing I remember is looking into your tiny red face, so strong and new, and knowing that I would never accomplish anything greater. Even though I knew that you would be fine without me, if I had been given a choice, I would never have left you."

"How could you possibly have known that I would be fine?"

Evelina's eyes twinkled. "Let's call it a mother's intuition. And I can tell you this: you will not only be fine; you will be great. I know it."

Jocelyn held out the last remaining perfume bottle. "I . . . I broke the rest. I'm sorry."

Evelina took it and dashed it to the floor. The bottle shattered like all the others. "I don't care. They weren't important. Not like you." She reached over and cradled Jocelyn in her arms. "I am the one who should be sorry."

Jocelyn allowed herself to be hugged for a long while before asking, "Can you stay?"

"I wish I could, but even fairy magic cannot bring the dead back to life. However, I can remain in this room for as long as you need. Time will not touch us here."

Time. Jocelyn thought of the ticking clock buried deep inside the Neverland's crocodile. All the girl's problems pressed in. Her father's request had not yet been fulfilled, her crew was at the mercy of the merciless Captain Krueger, and Roger . . . Jocelyn shook her head. As much as she felt comforted by her mother, she wondered if she had wasted her fairy wish. "I don't know what to do."

"The first step is to decide what you really want."

"I want to do what my father expects of me."

"James is dead and expects nothing." Evelina seated

herself on the bed, patting a spot beside her. "What do you want for yourself?"

Jocelyn sat, pulling her bare feet beneath her. "If I don't finish this business with the crocodile, I will live with the failure my whole life. I want to succeed, but I don't know if I'm strong enough."

"You are. You have a power within you even greater than all the magic of the fairies."

"No offense," Jocelyn replied. "You probably do know a lot, being from another realm or something, but I've met the fairies. You have no idea how powerful they are."

Evelina laughed. "Oh, Jocelyn, children are ever so much more powerful. The proof is simple. What happens when a child says, 'I don't believe in fairies'?"

That Evelina, she was a clever one. She must have known that all children, with the exception of a few addlepated simpletons, can answer that question in their sleep. Listen up, so you can be sure to get it.

"Every time a child says, 'I don't believe in fairies,' a fairy falls down dead," Jocelyn recited.

"Something similar happens when a child turns that doubt inward. The part of her that can do anything fades away. In time, and fed enough disbelief, it will die."

Jocelyn wasn't sure if she agreed, but she listened anyway.

"The crocodile feeds on fear and doubt. A few years

ago you would have been able to defeat it without much difficulty, but now more uncertainties have crept in. In order to get what you want, you must find a way to push them back."

Jocelyn pulled at a ragged thread on her sleeve. "That's the big secret? Believe in myself and everything will turn out fine? That sounds . . . stupid."

Evelina laughed. "That doesn't make it untrue. Or easy, as I'm certain you will discover. It holds the key to anything you may wish to accomplish, not just defeating the crocodile. You must look within yourself to discover what you really want, believe that you can have it, and not allow anything to keep you from it." She smoothed a lock of Jocelyn's hair, tucking it behind an ear. "Rest now. You have a difficult task ahead of you."

Jocelyn snuggled down into the bed, drowsiness settling over her like a comforting blanket. Her mother's cool hand caressed her forehead. Evelina began to hum a lullaby, and the girl closed her eyes. When she opened them, she was back in the forest, the stillness only broken by the sweet song of a nightingale.

"Decide what I want. Believe I can have it. Don't let anything stop me," the girl repeated to herself as she stood and started up the path.

Jocelyn wanted to rescue her crew and to defeat the crocodile. She was determined to do those things, but there was one thing she needed to do first—something she wanted above all else.

Jocelyn had to find Roger. He might choose to end their friendship, but he would do so remembering her.

CHAPTER THIRTY-SIX

Lost and Found

Jocelyn didn't know where to look for Roger, but she thought the fairies might have an idea. "Meriwether!" she called as she walked along, hoping the little prince would come.

Unlike humans, fairies only have room for one emotion at a time. We are a much more varied species. For example, when I look at you I am filled with many emotions—distaste, irritation, apoplectic rage—but fairies are simply not big enough for such complexities.

Meriwether was too filled with joy at Jocelyn's call to hold a grudge over her choosing to remain human. He flew straight for the girl, alighting on her outstretched hand. She was glad to see his damaged wing was nearly healed, though she was not quite as happy to find his desire for kisses had remained unchanged.

"Meriwether, stop that. I need your help. Can you show me how to find the lost boys?" He nodded and zipped through the trees, up a trail to the Mysterious River. Jocelyn followed as they traveled with the current, mostly uphill. After a time they arrived at a deep pool whence an upward-flowing waterfall crashed and roared as it ascended a rocky cliff.

The girl stared in wonder, only tearing her eyes away when Meriwether gave a gentle tug on her ear. He pointed up the bank, where Roger and the other lost boys were stomping around in the brush.

Roger bent over to examine a plant of some sort. In the short time since she had seen him last, he'd changed, now looking even less like the boy she knew. He was wearing a leaf-and-moss vest with pants made of coarse, dark fur. Looking closer, Jocelyn detected a new wildness about him that had nothing to do with his clothing.

The boy straightened, wiping his hands on his pants. They met each other's eyes. He smiled his familiar smile, waved, and motioned for her to join him. Jocelyn felt hope crack open a door inside her chest. She tried (but utterly failed) to keep some composure as she ran to him.

"Hello, girl. Want to have another berry fight?" he called over the rush of the waterfall.

The hopeful door slammed shut. "No, I don't want to have a berry fight! Roger, listen to me. You have to try to remember."

"Very well. Remember what?" Meriwether flitted about Roger's head, making rude gestures. "Is this your fairy? Peter has a fairy."

"Meriwether, stop that!" she said. He settled onto her shoulder, wings tickling her neck.

One of the lost boys, still wearing his torn jackalope hood, joined them. He scowled at Jocelyn but did not otherwise acknowledge her. Holding up an acorn, he asked, "Is this it, Dodge?"

Roger shook his head. "No, sorry, Ace. That's an acorn. It won't do anything to the pirates."

"Are there pirates nearby?" Jocelyn asked, thinking of her lost crew.

"Certainly," Roger said. "Their ship is harbored right over there." He motioned vaguely up the waterfall. "Or at least it was this morning."

"How about this, Dodge? Is this it?" the chubby boy yelled from where he stood, holding up a rock.

"No, Fredo, that's a rock!" Roger called back to him. He chuckled and went back to searching through the undergrowth.

Jocelyn tried again. "Roger—"

"It's Dodge." He didn't even look up.

"No, it's Roger! And I'm Jocelyn."

"Hi, Jocelyn." He sounded just as he always had. He couldn't be completely gone.

"Roger. Try to remember. What about the school? Miss Eliza Crumb-Biddlecomb's Finishing School for Young Ladies?"

He shrugged. "That doesn't seem like the kind of school I would go to."

"You weren't a student. You worked there: cook's helper, undergardener, and all-around errand boy?"

He continued his search, moving a bit away from her. "That sounds like a fun game."

"It wasn't a game!" she shouted.

"You are very grumpy this morning. Did you have breakfast?"

"No, why?"

"I don't know. I thought you might get short-tempered when you don't get enough to eat. I wish I had some food in my pocket, but I don't. These bearskin pants didn't even have pockets when Peter gave them to me, but I gave two purple beetles to a gnome tailor and—"

The twins called out in unison, "Look, Dodge! We think we've got it." They held up a pair of brown turtles.

"No, Twin and Twin," Roger said. "We're searching for a fruit, remember? A green fruit with purple spikes. Boys, come over here." He pulled a crumpled piece of paper from his pocket. "Look at this." All the boys gathered around. Jocelyn stood at the edge of the circle, feeling very small and alone. "See," Roger said, "devil's apple. There's a picture right here. Spread out and keep looking."

Jocelyn craned her neck to get a look at what he was holding. It was the page she had torn from *Impress Your Friends, Confound Your Enemies: 1001 Poisonous Jungle Plants and How to Use Them.* She could see her apology, written on one side. "That's my note! Where did you get it?"

Roger scratched his head. "I don't think it's yours. A bird gave it to me a few days ago."

"That was Edgar. I asked him to deliver it. I tore a page from your book so I could write to you. Think, Roger! Can you remember the carriage house at school? We went there to read and dream about having grand adventures someday."

Roger knit his eyebrows together. "Aren't we having adventures now?"

"We are, but this isn't the way it was supposed to work out. We were supposed to go together. You promised! But then Miss Eliza thought that we ... that I ..."

"Who is Miss Eliza? Is she here too?" He looked around. "I don't think I like her very much."

"That's right, Roger, you don't. She sent you away to a dreadful place and said we couldn't be friends."

"That wasn't very nice." He was still frowning.

Jocelyn felt a lump in her throat. "No, no it wasn't.

When I tried to find you, to tell you that I was sorry, you were already gone. That's why I sent the note."

"Why were you sorry? What did you do?" he asked.

This was hard to talk about. Jocelyn checked to see where the rest of the lost boys were. They had spread out along the river and the edge of the forest—too far to hear, even if there hadn't been a roaring waterfall masking her voice. Meriwether's wings tickled Jocelyn's neck again. She shooed him away. He flew off and settled on a nearby limb, arms folded, with his back to her, the very picture of a sulky fairy.

Jocelyn cleared her throat. "If I..." Her mouth felt dry. She swallowed and began again. "If I hadn't needed you so much, if I had left you alone, you wouldn't have been sent away."

Roger grinned at her, though not quite in the just-for-her way Jocelyn wished to see. "So, if you had decided not to be my friend, this Eliza person couldn't have stopped us from being friends." He nudged her with his elbow. "Sounds like you did something terrible, for certain."

What Roger said made sense. Some of Jocelyn's guilt fell away, only to be replaced with more sadness. Roger, *her* Roger, was right there in front of her, acting the same friendly way he always had, but he didn't know her.

"Anyway," the boy continued, "if you want to have an adventure, you can help us find some devil's apple. We're going to make a drink for the pirates. It probably won't kill them, but it might make them think they are seeing ghosts or something. All except that one with the eye patches, I suppose. Perhaps he would hear ghosts, though."

Absorbed as she was in her desire to make Roger remember, it took a moment for his words to sink in. *The one with the eye patches?* "Is he on the ship you were talking about?" Perhaps, by some miracle, her men had not been captured at all.

Roger slapped at a mosquito, still intent on his hunt for the poison. "Oh yes. Him, a pirate with one arm, a portly one that cries all the time, and a couple others."

"And they aren't prisoners? They're all right?"

"No, they're not anyone's prisoners. And they'll be all right until we give them some devil's-apple juice. We are at war with them, you know."

"Meriwether," Jocelyn called. The fairy crossed his eyes and stuck out his tongue at her. "Fine, then, if you don't want to do something special, just for me." Jocelyn gave what she hoped was a coaxing smile. "Something that no one else could do . . ."

Meriwether rocketed over and began making a nest in the girl's hair.

"All right. All right. Stop that. I need you to fly up the cliff and see if you can find the *Hook's Revenge* in the harbor. She will be flying a black flag with a red hook. Will you do that for me?" He nodded his head, bells ringing joyfully, and shot out of sight.

Jocelyn turned back to Roger. "I thought that Krueger had captured them."

He stopped digging through the bushes and sat back on his heels. "Is Krueger an evil-looking pirate with a scar on his face and pointy teeth?"

Jocelyn nodded. "Have you seen him?"

Roger shivered. "Yeah. The ones in the harbor—your men? They were fighting him a couple nights ago, in the storm. Peter heard there was a pirate battle, so we drew lots to pick a side. After we helped your pirates win—"

"You helped my men defeat Krueger? How?"

"Oh, that was easy. Peter let us use some of Tink's fairy dust and we all flew out to the battle. If you can fly, and those you are fighting cannot, well . . . that puts them at quite a disadvantage, you know."

Jocelyn scowled, remembering her dream where that flying Peter Pan so unfairly fought with her father. But if Pan and his lost boys—and Roger—had helped her men fight off Krueger, she couldn't be too irritated, could she? "So you killed Krueger and his men?" she asked, unsure of what she wanted the answer to be.

"Killed them? Oh no. At least, I don't think so. We pushed a few into the water, but their ship was only a short swim away. I know the captain made it aboard for certain. I saw him climbing up a loose rope, looking angrier than a wet cat."

Jocelyn shivered at the thought of Krueger, out there somewhere, possibly plotting his revenge.

"Anyway," Roger went on, "after we helped your pirates win the battle, Peter declared war on them, but he didn't want to fight them the same old way we fought the others. He told us to think up a new plan while he finds out what side Tiger Lily wants to be on. We decided to poison them. That is, if we can find the apples."

The lost boys were gone now, off searching in the thick foliage surrounding them. Roger walked closer to the river. "I don't think it's a water plant, but my information cuts off in the middle of the description."

Jocelyn moved between him and the water. She grabbed him by the shoulders. "Roger!" she shouted over the roar of the waterfall. "Try to remember who you were before you came here. Please! Try to remember me!"

He stared hard at her face. "I . . . I . . ." His eyes drifted from her face to a spot behind her and grew wide. "Watch out!" he yelled, and shoved her to the side.

Jocelyn fell hard, banging her elbow on a rock. She turned her head toward the river. The crocodile was clawing its way up the muddy bank, coming straight for her. Only now, when it was nearly upon her, could Jocelyn hear a clock tick-tocking over the sound of the waterfall.

The girl tried to pull her sword from its scabbard, but

she was lying on it. She struggled to get to her feet, to free her sword, to fight, but wasn't fast enough. From off to her right, a rock flew toward the beast, crashing into its side with a hollow thud.

"Run, girl!" Roger called to her.

With a deep, reptilian snarl the beast turned toward him and lunged. A pair of massive jaws caught the boy by his leg and began pulling him toward the water. Roger's scream was alive with pain and terror.

Jocelyn scrambled to her feet, positioning herself between the monster and the river. "Let him go!" she commanded, ignoring her fear. Still holding Roger in its jaws, the beast turned a half circle, now parallel to the river. Jocelyn drew her sword. It backed away, dragging her now-silent friend in the direction of the forest.

"I said let him go!" she shouted again, leaping forward. She lashed out with her sword, striking the monster in the soft area behind its front leg. Her blow did not puncture the skin, but it did appear to cause the monster some pain. With a low growl, it dropped its captive and retreated into the trees. Once the crocodile's ticktock had faded completely, Jocelyn looked down.

Roger lay at her feet, crumpled and still.

CHAPTER THIRTY-SEVEN

It Is Poor Manners to Play with Your Food

Jocelyn knelt in the mud, cradling Roger's head in her lap. He was breathing, but he lay unnaturally still. "Help!" she screamed. "Somebody help me!"

There are many advantages to having your own dearly devoted fairy—not least of all a friend willing to come to your aid whenever you call. That is, if they feel like it. Sometimes they are busy doing other things, like studiously ignoring you or finding ways to make you miserable. In that way, fairy friends are not much different from human ones.

Meriwether must have felt like heeding Jocelyn's call. He appeared at her side even faster than the lost boys, though they too crashed out of the forest in response to her cries.

"Was my ship in the harbor?" the girl asked her fairy. Meriwether nodded.

"Is there any way you can help this boy get aboard?" He nodded again and pulled a tiny reed pipe from his vest. When he blew on it, Jocelyn heard only a sound like wind through trees, but it must have been a royal summons. In an instant, a small army of fairy soldiers descended from the sky and surrounded Roger's still form. They showered him, and everything else nearby, with a cloud of glowing fairy dust. Jocelyn sneezed and rubbed it out of her eyes.

Roger's troubled expression smoothed into a small smile. Still sleeping, he floated off the ground. The fairies easily conducted him over the trees toward the harbor.

"Go with them," Jocelyn commanded the lost boys, "in case he needs something."

"Where are you going, girl?" Fredo asked.

Jocelyn didn't answer. She scanned the ground until she found what she needed. Without a word, she set off, following the monster's track.

For her friend, she would find a way to stop time itself.

We are nearly there: the point where I will have finished spilling my guts and you will leave before I am tempted to spill yours.

The Neverland may have sensed Jocelyn's determination to confront its monster one last time, but it did not give her easy passage. Clouds of tiny flies swarmed in front of her face, making it difficult to see. The trail narrowed and trees joined dark arms above her head, hiding the sun behind a ragged curtain of moss. The ground grew damp, then marshy. Stinking black mud sucked at her bare feet. The very air tried to impede the girl's progress, growing still and heavy with the stifling scent of rot.

There are a few places in this world where darkness pools and fears come alive. The Neverland has such a spot: the Black Swamp. As it was a place particularly well suited to the malignant nature and appetite of the crocodile, this was where the monster chose to make its home. Jocelyn followed its trail, clear in the wet ground, leading directly to its dark den.

After a time, the path widened, though little light shone down. The heart of the swamp was grim and dank and utterly bereft of life. Even the flies were gone. There, in the stillness, only the ticktock of a clock filled the air. As before, back in the carriage house, Jocelyn's heart sounded in time.

She stood at the edge of an oily black bog. Barren trees, bent and broken, struggled to rise from the fetid depths. The water, thick and dark as congealed blood, bubbled and belched noxious fumes. It brought to Jocelyn's mind thoughts of witches bent over their terrible cauldrons. In the center of the poisonous brew, the crocodile lurked, red eyes just visible above the murk.

The girl's voice sounded braver than she felt. "You took my father. You took my courage. And you nearly took my friend." She held up her sword in a shaky fist. "I will not let you have another chance. You will not steal from me again. Come out and face me." Without any other movement, the monster turned a bloodred eye to the girl. Sheer malice radiated from its gaze, and Jocelyn staggered back.

Wicked laughter erupted all around her, catching the girl by surprise. She kept her eyes on the beast, but her voice trembled as she called, "Who's there?"

Near a line of trees bordering the foul marsh, faint, misty figures took form. Jocelyn wondered if they were ghosts—perhaps the spirits of the crocodile's victims? One spectral image drifted forward. Jocelyn could see, through its body, the dark and broken trees behind it.

The apparition addressed the girl. "Look at the little hero, playing at bravery." Its voice dripped sarcasm directly into her ear. Goose bumps erupted on Jocelyn's skin.

The others laughed and repeated: "...playing at bravery."

Jocelyn furrowed her brow, intent on the shape coming into focus before her. "I know you! You're Prissy Edgeworth! Or at least you were." Just as she always had at school, Pinch-Face appeared at Prissy's side. "What are you two doing here? Did you die?"

The ghost girl smirked at her. "Death did not create us. We are the images that you keep in your head." She giggled. "Only we got out."

"How?"

"It is the power of this place. The Black Swamp is home to what you fear most. That is the reason the monster brought you here. Why, look for yourself—he's already gorging himself on you."

Jocelyn reluctantly turned her gaze to the beast lurking in the dark water. Perhaps it was only her imagination, but the crocodile, at least as much of it as Jocelyn could see, seemed to grow larger before her eyes. A chill ran down her spine, but she put on a brave face.

More specters joined those already gathered. They grew more solid, nearly as real as life. "Look at her, Nanette," the phantom Prissy said to the figure beside her. "Jocelyn Hook, the girl hero, is going to slay this gigantic beast and carry its head triumphantly back to school. Perhaps Miss Eliza will have it mounted and hung above the mantel. That will put us in our place."

"...in our place," Nanette and the others echoed back.

"That's right! I will. Just watch me." Jocelyn looked at the beast again. It hadn't moved, but she couldn't fight it in the water. Why didn't it come to her?

"Now, now, girls." A third figure floated forward. "We must remember that Miss Hook is the offspring of the infamous Captain Hook." Jocelyn recognized the features of Miss Eliza on the specter's face. "Though I'd be surprised if you had forgotten; she does so often remind us. Pity that she will never live up to his legacy."

"My father was the most feared man that ever lived. I will prove myself to him—to all of you!"

Next it was her grandfather, Sir Charles, gliding toward her. "Young lady, this is utter foolishness! You were meant to become a fine society lady, though that is obviously a hopeless proposition. You are nothing but a disappointment."

"You are nothing. You are a disappointment." The figures flew to the girl, circling her as they laughed—mocking, pulling at her hair and clothes. She flung her arms up over her face and screamed. If Jocelyn could have seen the beast at that instant, she would have noticed an evil grin upon its foul mouth. It so enjoyed playing with its food. It drifted closer to her now, as though its hunger was growing.

The specters grew still, but they did not release the girl from where she stood, captive in their midst. Directly in front of her, at the head of the circle hedging her in, floated her grandfather and Miss Eliza. They pulled aside, creating a gap.

Jocelyn's knees went weak. She could not believe what she was seeing.

Through the gap strode Captain Hook himself.

CHAPTER THIRTY-EIGHT

In Which Time Stops

Jocelyn took in the fine cut of her father's impeccable clothing, the wicked gleam of his iron hook. His face was wreathed with black curls, not wild and tangled like hers, but restrained, controlled. The very swamp bent to his command. He was immune to the mud that sucked and pulled at Jocelyn's feet. Hook strolled right over it, not even sullying his polished black boots. Jocelyn focused on their shine, reluctant to look into his eyes, afraid of what might be there—and what might be missing.

"So you took up the challenge." His deep, rich voice held the edge of a sneer. "I didn't expect you would."

Jocelyn spoke past the lump forming in her throat. "You asked me to. Your letter said it was my inheritance."

"Indeed I did. You were to come and avenge me. Fine job you've made of it too. You are a failure."

Finally, she brought her eyes to his. They were shockingly blue, deep and cold, like the open sea. "This is not over. I will kill the crocodile."

Hook let out a hard, bitter laugh. "I was the most feared man to ever live. Flint feared me. The Sea-Cook feared me. Blackbeard learned to fear me. I made Kidd, Morgan, and Rackham wet themselves like children. And yet, that . . . *crocodile*"—Hook spat out the word like wormy salt pork—"that creature *killed* me! Me! Captain James Hook, terror of the seas! How do you, a mewling infant, expect to defeat it when you are nothing but a mere girl?"

The ring of specters looked on in silent judgment. Meanwhile, the crocodile drew closer through the inky water. It ignored Hook, its bloodred eyes focused instead on the trembling girl. If the monster fed on despair, the scent wafting off her must have been delectable. It had taken its time, seasoning its intended meal with fear like a delicate sauce. It would not wait much longer.

"Because . . ." Jocelyn faltered. She thought on her mother's words. "Because I believe I can." It came out sounding like a question.

"'Because I believe I can,'" Hook mocked. "How like a little girl. 'All you need do is believe in yourself, and you can do anything.' What absolute drivel!"

"It's true!" Jocelyn cried. "My mother told me it was true."

"Mothers lie, girl! That is their principal occupation. Nothing will save you. That crocodile will bite and chew and swallow and there will be nothing left to you and no one to mourn your passing."

"That's not true!"

"Who cares for you?"

"My crew—"

"Your crew is a pack of fools not fit to brush my jacket—and even they only follow you because of my name! You are not worthy to be called by it. No one fears or admires you. Your grandfather sent you away; your only friend forgot you. I rarely thought of you myself, and when I did, it was with disdain. And your precious mother? She did not care even the minuscule amount it would have taken for her to live. She did not *have* to die, you know. She left you."

"Stop it!" Jocelyn cried, sudden tears stinging her eyes. "My mother loved me."

"Ah, becoming emotional, how trite. Bad form, girl, bad form. This is why you so often fail. Because you are nothing like me."

Jocelyn tried to summon her bravery. "Like *you*? You do not exist! None of you do. You are only weak copies of the people I know." Jocelyn said the words, and she tried to believe them. The girl looked around the circle of misty figures, concentrating on their faces. She knew each one well: household servants, girls from school; shockingly, even Smee and the rest of her pirate crew flashed spiteful grins at her. Most hurtful of all was the appearance of Roger, his easy laughter now full of mockery.

Her father spoke, pointing at her with his fearsome hook. "No one believes in you." It was nearly a whisper, but it pierced Jocelyn to the heart.

The circle repeated it loudly, joyfully: "No one believes in you!"

Jocelyn had suspected it all along, but to hear it stated so bluntly hurt more than she was willing to admit. "You lie!"

He ignored her. "Then where are your precious friends? Where is your crew? They have abandoned you. Even your lost boy did not return to stand at your side."

Roger.

"You came here to avenge my death. You came here to be a great pirate captain. But all you have done is flit about the Neverland, frolicking with mermaids..."

The mermaids.

"...giving lessons in manners..."

The cannibals.

"...and playing with your own pet fairy." At this her father swiped at her with his hook, sending up a shower of excess fairy dust still clinging to her clothes.

My own fairy. If Meriwether is mine, Jocelyn thought, *it is only because I saved him.*

Hook's cruel words cut Jocelyn to the core, but what they finally struck there was made of steel. She had had enough. The girl brushed aside her tears. "You are right. I am not like you." She took a step toward the figure of her father. "I am young. I am a girl. I prefer rumpled to refined. I use poor manners, when they are called for."

As she spoke these words, the image of Hook grew slightly less substantial. "My compassion, of which you have none, led me to kill the snake and free Meriwether. That made him mine."

She stood straighter, the burden her father had placed upon her weighing less heavily now. "My song softened the cold heart of a mermaid. My wit allowed me to trick the cannibals and escape. I did all of these things on my own. You are not even real." At these words, Hook's figure grew quite faint; she could see the skeletal trees behind him. She looked around the circle. "None of you are real!" The other specters were no more than misty outlines now. She could see through all of them.

"I saved Roger"—she stepped right through the insubstantial images that had held her captive and faced the crocodile, now only feet away from the edge of the shore—"from you. You will be the one to fail today."

Jocelyn raised herself to her full height and pointed her

sword at the monster. "Dark and sinister beast, prepare to meet your doom."

The image of her father, and all the other specters, dissipated as the crocodile snarled with rage, its eyes locked on hers.

From the other side of the clearing came the song of a nightingale. It was joined by a tinkling of bells, crashing of bracken, happy weeping, and shouting:

"I hear our young captain. If my ears can be believed, and they certainly can, she is but a few footfalls away!"

"Cap'n, we don't care if we were banished. We're coming!"

"I think it's this way! What do you think, Twin?"

Once again, figures broke through the line of trees, only these had far more substance than the swamp's ghostly apparitions. Jocelyn's heart filled with happiness. Prince Meriwether and his regiment of fairy soldiers flew out of the mist, escorting Mr. Smee, along with the rest of the girl's own pirate crew (with the exception of Dirty Bob, who had been left behind to guard the ship). The lost boys followed, armed with a basket full of rotten berries. Roger led the company, leaning slightly on Blind Bart. The boy was obviously still weak, but he was on his feet, eyes shining with excitement.

Jocelyn tingled with warmth. She had never felt lighter, never freer than this moment. The scattered fairy dust coating her skin glowed in the gloom. She shouted with joy and cast off the tethers that held her to the earth.

Jocelyn lifted her feet and flew.

She laughed, soaring high above the brackish swamp, up where the wind was sweet and cool. The crocodile erupted in a mass of fury. It lunged into the air, jaws snapping furiously, but Jocelyn only soared higher, calling, "You'll have to do better than that if you want to catch me, you old codfish!"

The monster snarled with rage, rancid spittle flying from its gaping maw. It sprang again, this time catching the hem of the girl's dress in its jaws, its jagged teeth barely skimming her ankle. Jocelyn jerked back, tearing her dress away, and rewarded the beast by giving it a hard slap on the snout with the flat of her blade. The creature's red eyes rolled in their sockets, wild with pain and anger. Jocelyn's friends cheered as the crocodile landed with a splash in the black water and sank below the surface.

She waited. One heartbeat. Two. It did not reappear. Jocelyn dipped down, skimming the swamp's surface, searching. The ticking was still present, but faint. The entire swamp bubbled, making it difficult to pinpoint where the monster was hiding. She bent her head to investigate a series of ripples.

From behind her, the beast's powerful tail rose out of the water. It smashed into the girl, sending her spinning through the air. She crashed into a broken tree at the edge of the water and fell to the ground. The crocodile lurched out of the swamp after her. Jocelyn's friends rushed forward, but she stood and waved them off.

It was time to end this. And she would do it on her own.

The monster lunged. Jocelyn twirled around and slipped under it, graceful as a dancer, with her sword upheld. The crocodile came down on her weapon, which buried itself to the hilt in the creature's reptilian breast. Metal struck metal as Jocelyn's blade pierced the old clock, silencing its tick forever.

Inky blackness poured from the ragged hole in the beast's chest, surrounding Jocelyn in a wicked cloud, blinding her to everything else, but she merely scowled at the gloom, waving it away. The darkness released her, gathering itself into the shadow of a man.

A man with a hook instead of a right hand.

The shadow nodded at the girl. She curtsied back.

A soft breeze blew into the swamp, carrying with it a salty tang of sea air. The shadow lost form and scattered on the wind. At Jocelyn's feet lay the remains of the Neverland's fearsome crocodile. She nudged it with her foot, bewildered by what she saw. It appeared as if the crocodile had been empty all along. Now it was only a deflated pile of skins, a broken clock, and an iron hook.

The girl turned to her cheering friends, locking eyes with Roger. He gave a little bow. "Well done—Jocelyn, is it? Even Peter Pan and we lost boys combined couldn't have done better." He smiled at her then, in a not-quite-the-just-for-her way, but still very nice.

Perhaps Roger did not remember the past, but that did not mean they could have no future.

Jocelyn dropped her sword and ran to her new, old friend, giving him an affectionate elbow to the stomach. He laughed and rubbed dirt on her face before pulling her into an awkward, but sweet, hug.

Jocelyn basked in a warm feeling of relief. It may not have been in the way she had hoped, but it was enough. Roger had returned to her.

CHAPTER THIRTY-NINE

"Oh, the Cockiness of Me!"

Jocelyn stood over the pile of empty crocodile skins. She had done it. She had really done it. Mr. Smee placed a hand on her shoulder. "Well now, look at that. A sight that even your father might have been proud to see, miss, though not nearly as pleased as me." His voice broke and he sniffed loudly. "Do any of you lot have a handkerchief? I have a touch of the hay fever."

Jocelyn tore a strip of fabric from her ruined hem and handed it to the man. "There, there, Mr. Smee. There, th—"

Her words of comfort were interrupted by Fredo, the chubby lost boy, calling out, "Peter is coming! Look, Ace, Peter is coming!" He pointed to the sky, where Peter Pan zigged and zagged over the tops of trees, making a show of his approach.

Jocelyn's pirate crew, with the exception of Smee, ran off into the bushes. "Don't tell Peter we are here! We are supposed to be banished!" the retreating form of One-Armed Jack called out.

"Go after my men and bring them back!" Jocelyn commanded Smee. "Tell them I said not to care about that boy—that they are under both my command and my protection. Remind them that *I* am their captain."

Smee wiped a tear from his eye. "Aye, that you are, miss. That you are." He crashed off through the bracken, yelling, "Get over here, you lily-livered deserters, or I'll have your heads!" Eager to be of assistance, Meriwether and his regiment of soldiers followed along.

A moment later, Peter arrived, accompanied by a tiny ball of light darting about his head. Jocelyn rolled her eyes. He had brought his fairy.

The boy hovered over what remained of the beast and crowed, "The great Neverland crocodile is dead. Oh, the cleverness of me!" His fairy settled onto his shoulder and clapped her hands in a show of appreciation.

Jocelyn glowered at them both. "What on earth do you mean, 'the cleverness of me'? You had nothing to do with it!"

"Of course I did! The crocodile was the Neverland's

most fearsome beast. It is now dead. I must have killed it. Cock-a-doodle-do!"

"Stop making that ridiculous noise." She placed her hands on her hips and stomped her foot. "You did no such thing! I killed the monster."

"You? But you are a girl." Peter laughed so hard he nearly fell out of the sky. His fairy joined in, bells ringing mirthfully. Jocelyn reached for her sword, but Roger put a gentle hand on her arm.

"It had to have been me," Peter went on. "Right, lost boys?"

The lost boys gave one another bewildered looks. Ace shrugged, making his dangling jackalope horns bob, and said, "Sure you did, Peter. Didn't he, Fredo?"

Fredo scratched his head and replied, "Yup. He did. It was fantastic—right, Twin?"

Both twins nodded. "The best battle we ever saw," they replied in unison. "Don't you think so, Dodge?"

Roger looked from Peter to Jocelyn and back again. "Absolutely," he replied.

Jocelyn glared at him and pulled her arm from his grasp, but he winked at her and continued: "I've never seen anything like it. When Captain Jocelyn Hook killed the crocodile, she did it with style. Certainly the best battle I ever saw." Turning to face the girl directly, he added, "Pretty fine dancing, Jocelyn. Were those your own steps or ones you learned from Gerta?" His smile grew into the very one Jocelyn had been missing. Roger knew her!

She might have sobbed with joy and relief, if Peter hadn't interrupted. (For that, we can give him our grudging gratitude.)

"Silence, you!" he gnashed his teeth. "For siding with the girl and consorting with pirates, henceforth and forevermore you are banished! How do you like that, Dodge?"

Roger gave the boy a slow smile. "I like it all right. And my name isn't Dodge—it's Roger. I am a lost boy no more." He turned his gaze to Jocelyn. "Not lost at all."

Jocelyn slipped her hand into Roger's. She hardly gave the leader of the lost boys, and the Neverland's wonder, a glance.

"Go home, Peter Pan, you silly boy. We've no use for you just now."

A shrill alarm sounded, and a streak of light flew at the girl's face, aiming for her eyes. Meriwether crashed out of the surrounding foliage and intercepted it. The two fairies tumbled through the air, furiously ringing like the harness bells on a runaway horse. The prince's royal fairy army followed him, surrounding the pair. Four soldiers wrestled the fuming fairy girl away, and the entire regiment escorted her off. Meriwether stayed behind, settling onto Jocelyn's upturned hand.

Peter stared, pop-eyed and mouth agape.

"That's right, Pan," Jocelyn said. "I have a fairy."

The boy drifted down to the ground. "You . . . you . . . you CODFISH!" He hurled the insult at Jocelyn and gathered his boys around him. "Come on, lost boys. Good-bye, *girl*."

Fredo, Ace, and the twins waved to Jocelyn and joined their leader.

"That's *Captain* Girl to you," she called after Peter, as he led his lost boys up the path, clinging tightly to the last remaining shreds of his dignity.

There you have it. That is the tale of how young Captain Jocelyn Hook, daughter of the most feared pirate to ever live, managed to face her own fears, survive the Neverland, defeat a monster, and find her lost boy—all without having to brush her hair.

Jocelyn succeeded, and did it her own way.

Now please quit pestering me and leave. I have things to do.

Go Away

CHAPTER FORTY

*Wherein the Narrator Feels
Utterly Harassed*

NOW, where did I put my Sunday cutlass? It
wants polishing.

What, are you still here? Very well. I suppose you still have a few questions. Perhaps you want to
know why the crocodile was empty?

That should be easy for any thinking person to guess—
but I'll spell it out for you.

After the crocodile swallowed the hand of Captain
James Hook, the vile toxins in the pirate's blood—as
Mr. Smee had correctly surmised—went to work on
the poor, dumb beast. That bit of Hook digesting in its
belly burned like an acid, eating away the crocodile's soft
insides and creating a dark hole. From what I understand,
the creature mistook that hole inside itself for hunger—a

hunger that could only be satisfied by devouring the rest of the pirate. Once it had achieved this end, the poison in Hook's blood ate away at the rest of the beast, leaving only an iron hook, an empty shell, and a malicious will.

Oh yes, and the clock, of course.

That clock was made of metal and was therefore impervious to the effects of the acidic toxin. In fact, if you'll remember correctly, the clock had not been ticking when the crocodile finally caught Hook. Its silence had allowed the beast to sneak up on the doomed man and take him to his final resting place within its guts. Some say the clock had wound down, but I believe it had rusted from sitting so long in the damp belly of the crocodile. The amount of acid the creature ingested when it made a meal of Captain Hook was certainly enough to clean and polish the clock, starting it ticking once again.

There you have it.

The Story Is Now Over
I mean it this time. Go away.

Can't you see we are finished here? Why have you not left?

What do you mean, "What happened to Jocelyn?" She killed the crocodile; weren't you listening?

Oh, *after*, you mean.

Jocelyn commanded Roger and her crew to return to the *Hook's Revenge* for an impromptu victory party. There they celebrated, stories were exchanged, songs were sung, and more than a few tears were shed. Then Smee wiped his eyes and got to work making each man a pair of crocodile boots (except for Nubbins, who requested a new chef's apron).

The young captain found a quiet corner away from her celebration to talk with Roger. "I could hardly believe it when I saw you, well and whole, in the swamp. I had been so worried that the crocodile had—" She swallowed, the words stuck in her throat. "How is your leg?"

"A little bruised, but otherwise fine. Never underestimate the power of bearskin pants." His eyes twinkled. "Bearskin pants—with pockets. Thank you for returning this." He held up his compass. "Though I'm afraid it may not work all that well. Even with this most excellent tool, I was still lost for too long. I am sorry about that."

Jocelyn shrugged. "You're not lost now. That's the important thing."

"When the crocodile came up out of the water—when it tried to attack you . . ." He shook his head. "I only knew that I couldn't let it hurt you. Then it grabbed me and the last thing I recall thinking was, 'Better me than her.' I woke on your ship and the first thing I thought of was you. I had this feeling . . . I don't know, somehow I knew you were important to me—but I couldn't remember why. Then, later, when I had to choose between you and Peter . . . You had been so brave and true and really, just magnificent, how could I deny that?"

Jocelyn shrugged. "I don't know."

"I couldn't. I chose you. And I suddenly remembered the day we first met, you were soaking wet and covered in mud. You looked awful." He grinned. "No offense."

She smiled back at him. "None taken."

"On that day, I said I would be on your crew. We spit on our hands and made a deal, remember?"

Jocelyn nudged him with her shoulder. "Of course I do, you foolish boy."

Roger grinned at her. "After I remembered that, I remembered, well, everything—Miss Eliza's, the carriage house . . . Magellan." He gave a gentle tug to one of her curls, but then his face grew grave. "And something else, too. I remembered that you mean more to me than anyone."

Jocelyn looked straight into Roger's deep brown eyes, her heart pounding nearly as hard as when she'd faced the crocodile. She leaned toward him. "I feel the same—"

"I beg your pardon, miss," Smee interrupted, "but I wanted to give you these. It looked like you might be needing something, since you don't seem to have any shoes." He held out a pair of crocodile slippers.

Roger stood and addressed the night air. "Cats of the

Neverland, beware! Captain Jocelyn Hook is armed once more."

Jocelyn began to giggle. Roger joined in, egging her on. She grabbed him by the arm and yanked him back down to sit beside her. The two collapsed into fits of laughter while Mr. Smee looked on bemusedly.

Jocelyn couldn't remember a time when she felt such happiness. It was good to have her friend back.

Late in the night, Jocelyn tore herself away from her friends and crept off to her cabin. Meriwether rested on a shelf in the corner, giving a soft glow to the room. She riffled through her things until she found what she was looking for: a book of fairy tales. She tore a page from her least favorite story, Cinderella, and penned a note.

> Dear Mother,
> Whatever happens, I will be fine.
> Love from your daughter, Jocelyn

She folded it, placing it in her pocket. Tomorrow she would have Edgar deliver it to Evelina—sometime in the English When before she died.

The girl sat at the edge of her berth and picked up the last memento of her father—his iron hook. She thought of Hook's image in the clearing and the way it had mocked her. Jocelyn knew it had not really been her father, only a picture conjured by her own insecurities. Still, she did wonder how he might have felt about her, and how he would feel now.

Jocelyn turned her father's hook over in her hands, lost in thought. A tiny clinking sound interrupted her reverie. She held the hook to her ear and shook it. Something rattled inside. Running her fingers all over its cold surface revealed a small series of cracks, forming a rough square right on the part that would have pressed against her father's wrist.

Jocelyn used the hilt of her sword to give it a sharp tap. A thin piece of metal fell away, exposing a compartment hollowed into the hook's base. She turned it over, and a small but heavy object dropped into her open palm.

It was a key.

Jocelyn knew immediately the lock it would fit.

She knelt on the floor, pulling the chest of items her father had left her from under her bunk. She sifted through its contents until she found what she was looking for: the iron box engraved with a hook—though when she held it from a different angle, that hook looked like nothing more than a plain letter *J*.

Jocelyn fit the key in the lock and turned. The lid popped open, revealing the box's contents. On the top lay a tarnished silver rattle, engraved with the same *J*, and a plain gold band, large enough for a man's finger. Beneath them was a pile of papers, which Jocelyn removed and glanced over. There were several invoices from Edgar Allan's Mainland Courier Service, both for letters and a package: *Delivered—One Jeweled Locket*.

Jocelyn reached up and touched her necklace. "Thank you," she whispered.

One more paper, old and yellowing about the edges, lay at the bottom of the pile. Jocelyn gingerly unfolded it. It was a map. Across the top, in her father's bold hand, was scrawled *Captain Hook's Treasure*.

She ran her fingers across its surface. Her father's treasure.

"Weigh anchor, boys!" Jocelyn called out to her crew. "We're off on another adventure."

But that, you beetle-headed boob, is a story for another day.

This Is Really, Truly
The End

GLOSSARY OF PIRATE TERMS

Batten the Hatches Ships are built with hatches in the decking, leading to cargo space and crew quarters. During storms they are "battened" down or secured and made waterproof. "Batten the hatches" is often yelled by landlubbers pretending to be pirates. They generally have no idea what it means, but neither do those at whom it is yelled.

Now that you know its definition, you are at an advantage, perhaps the first in your young life. Do try not to waste it.

Belaying Pin A large and heavy wood pin used for securing ropes, though it also makes a handy weapon in a pinch. In addition to the more conventional uses, Nubbins once told me that he found it to be convenient for rolling out pastry dough for party dishes, but I'm rather certain he is the only pirate ever to have put one to that purpose. At any rate, it's quite a versatile tool.

Bilge The lowest part inside a ship. It is filthy, disgusting, and more often than not filled with trash, stagnant water, and rats. It isn't all bad, though: bilge rats are a good source of fresh meat at sea.

Bo'sun Shortened form of *boatswain*. It was likely shortened because the bo'sun has so much to do that he doesn't have time to say the whole word. He supervises the deck crew, oversees the ship's stores and provisions, and inspects the rigging, sails, chains, and anchors. In the case of Mr. Smee, the bo'sun also kept the captain's clothing in good repair, gave pep talks, and baked cakes—sometimes of the poisoned variety.

Bucko One who blusters, bullies, and bosses—generally an officer. Based on this description, some children might consider their mothers to be buckos, but I would not advise saying as much to her.

Cat-o'-Nine-Tails A lash made from nine knotted ropes. Also the only cat I like.

Clapped in Irons This kind of clapping does not mean applause. It refers to chaining up a prisoner—though I myself have done this with enough finesse to make onlookers cheer. Please let me know if you would like a personal demonstration.

Davy Jones/Davy Jones's Locker Davy Jones is the sailors' devil. His locker is the bottom of the sea. If you happen to drown in the ocean, your remains will be locked up tight there. Isn't that a nice thing to look forward to? For me, I mean.

Dog-Livered Landlubber A cowardly person who knows nothing about ships or the sea. In other words, you.

Dunking from the Yardarm A popular punishment at sea. The offending sailor is tied to a long rope and hauled high into the air to the yardarm, a part of the ship that supports the sail. Then the scoundrel is violently dropped into the sea—only to be hauled up and dunked again. I can't say it is particularly enjoyable for the dunkee, but if he survives, he might not need a bath again for a good long while. We must take whatever graces we can find at sea.

The Eye of the Wind The direction from whence the wind blows—useful knowledge aboard a vessel propelled by such. Blind Bart tried to make *ear of the wind* a saying, but it never caught on.

Flotsam and Jetsam Bits of floating wreckage or items cast overboard to stabilize a foundering ship. Also useless odds and ends, things, or people (for example, cats and children).

Galley The ship's kitchen, where such delicacies as hardtack and salt pork are dished out.

Hardtack and Salt Pork Common sea rations. Hardtack (also called sea biscuit) is a simple cracker that generally has the charming qualities of being both hard as rock and infested with weevils. It is a staple aboard pirate ships because most cooks, Nubbins excluded, like to believe that nearly everyone enjoys breaking his or her teeth on tasteless food filled with insects.

Salt pork is pork, preserved in barrels of salt—as should be obvious by the name.

Jolly Roger This phrase refers to more than Captain Hook's ship and Jocelyn's happy-go-lucky friend. *Jolly Roger* is also the name of a pirate flag, generally emblazoned with a skull and crossbones. Jocelyn embroidered a set of Jolly Roger napkins at school and gave them to Miss Eliza for Christmas. They were not much appreciated and never used.

Keelhauling Another pirate punishment. As in dunking from the yardarm, the offending sailor is tied to the end of a long rope with the other end attached to the ship. But instead of being dunked, he is tossed overboard and essentially run over, passing under the barnacle-encrusted keel (or main support) of the ship. Those razor-sharp barnacles give a rather vigorous scrubbing to the skin—one that puts even Gerta's ministrations to shame.

Disadvantage to the sailor: more likely than not, he will die.

Keep a Weather Eye To watch closely. Jocelyn, sensitive to Blind Bart's lack of vision (and because she felt bad that his *ear of the wind* campaign was not a success), amended the phrase to *weather ear*.

Marlinspike A wooden or metal tool used for rope work, and shaped like the nose of a swordfish (or marlin). Though the fish existed first, it was named *after* the marlinspike. I'd wager even your father doesn't know that.

Me Hearty "My friend." Take note of this. It is the first and last time you will ever find me saying those words to the likes of you.

Mutiny A conspiracy to overthrow the captain and take charge of the ship. Sometimes mutinous sailors kill the captain outright. Other times they show mercy, setting him adrift in a small boat with a supply of water and hardtack. At least he has the weevils to keep him company.

Offer No Quarter This means that no mercy will be given and no surrender will be accepted. The parties have to fight—to the death! Or, as it was in the Pirate and Lost Boy Wars, until they got tired and went home.

Poop Deck It may surprise you to learn that this term does not refer to a ship's bathroom. A ship's bathroom is called the *head*. Ships are interesting places.

The poop deck serves as the roof of the back, or aft, cabin. It is also from here that the ship is steered. On the *Hook's Revenge*, this was the highest decking area, which made it a good place for Captain Jocelyn to stand and address and/or berate her crew, as they needed and/or desired.

Powder Monkeys Pirates often use the term *monkey-sized* for any small thing. A powder monkey is a boy, just about your age, who carries gunpowder from the powder magazine, or room where it is stored, to the cannons. The only requirements of the job are being a small size (less easy for the enemy to target) and possessing enough wits to keep from blowing oneself up.

I'd recommend you for a position, but, though you are the right size, you are still underqualified.

ACKNOWLEDGMENTS

"To have faith is to have wings." J. M. Barrie, *The Little White Bird*

I am overwhelmed with gratitude for the many people who put their faith in this story and offered of themselves to lend it wings. There isn't space to list everyone who encouraged, lifted, taught, and inspired me, though gratitude to each is written in my heart.

Particular thanks to the following individuals:

Each person who read my manuscript and gave both astute advice and typo correction, including: Becky Clawson, Eve Nicholson, Laura and Senica Greaves, Michelle and McKenna Wonderling, and my dear SWs, thank you.

Additional thanks to Michelle and to Deon Sellers for being excellent understudies in the role of Mother. Thank you for the times you provided the fun so I could write without guilt.

Annie Cechini: inspirer, encourager, cheerleader, and the best paper-bag puppet maker I know. Thank you for loving this book so much I couldn't help but finish it.

Tyler Nevins for his book jacket design and John Hendrix for his amazingly detailed, wonderful, and beautiful illustrations for both the jacket and interior art. I am proud and thrilled that *Hook's Revenge* is dressed so finely.

My amazing editor, Rotem Moscovich. Jocelyn and Roger are ever so much happier now thanks to you, and to Julie Moody, Karen Sherman, and the rest of your team. It has been a true pleasure spending time on the Neverland with you all. I can't wait to return.

Brooks Sherman, how can I thank you enough? I joke that I let you be my agent but forced you to be my friend. I am so glad you are both. I will forever be grateful to you for saying yes to this story, for seeing what it could be, and for helping it become such. Here it is, Brooks, our first book! I look forward to many more together.

Hannah, my everything, who shows me every day what amazing looks like, who inspires me with her courage, creativity, and passion, and who never stopped asking when I was going to finish my/our book. It's done now, sweetheart. I hope you like it.

Walt, for all the dinners that I didn't make, all the laundry that I didn't fold, and the many, many ways every day that you encourage me to fly. On the day we married,

I told you, "What's yours is mine and what's mine is mine." Here is where I officially confess that I lied. I'm grateful to share it all with you. I love you forever. You will always be my one true home.

J. M. Barrie himself, creator of the boy who never grew up and the story that never grew old. I'm honored that my words have a tiny place in your Neverland.

And to you, dear reader. Thank you for spending this time with me. Let's do it again soon, shall we?

Yo ho!

Don't miss Jocelyn's next adventure!

Turn the page now for a sneak peek.

Secret Burdens

Secrets are tricky things. For many years, I was one of the few who knew about Captain Hook's daughter, Jocelyn, and the way she succeeded in avenging him upon the Neverland's monstrous crocodile. I held that knowledge close to my chest, gripping it tight as a new puppy, though at times the story wriggled and nipped, desperate to be put down.

There came a point where the burden grew too heavy. I thought that telling the world about the girl and her heroic victory would allow me some measure of relief, but it would not do. I have merely exchanged one affliction for another. Since I last had the misfortune of speaking to you, I am followed by throngs of children wherever I go. They reach for me with sticky hands, plead with lips stained by sweets, and constantly fill my ears with their unceasing, high-pitched refrain: "What happened next? Did Jocelyn find Hook's treasure?"

Even now, here you sit with your scabbed-over knees and insipid smile, waiting for me to tell you the tale. Without any effort, I can think of a dozen more pleasant ways to rid myself of your presence—ways that reduce you to nothing more than a stain and a memory—but still the remaining secrets I carry would demand to be released. And so, for my own sake, I must continue down this path and see it through to the bitter end.

It is true that Jocelyn's adventures did not end with the killing of the crocodile, nor with the return of her lost boy. There is more to be told. Much more.

Let's get this over with.

CHAPTER ONE

In Which Our Heroine Asks,
"What Could Go Wrong?"

There are many wonderful things about gold. The way it shines, the cool feel of it in one's hands, the sweet cries of those from whom you have stolen it . . . As far as I am concerned, there is only one undesirable thing about gold: not having enough of it.

Jocelyn was sorely feeling that one bad thing as she counted the remaining pieces of eight her father had left her. There were pitifully few, especially compared to the long list of needed supplies Mr. Smee had given her that morning.

She brushed the coins back into their bag with an irritated swipe of her hand. If only she could go after her father's treasure! It had been weeks since she killed the Neverland's crocodile and found her father's iron hook in its remains. A hollow section of the hook had held a key to a locked box Captain Hook had left in her possession—and within that box had lain a map to his vast treasure hoard.

It was rumored to be the greatest cache of treasure known to man, and Jocelyn felt anxious to find it. With even a portion of that gold, the girl would be captain of her own destiny. She wished that Mr. Smee, loyal bo'sun to both herself and her father before her, knew more about it, but Hook had never shown him the site of the treasure. Indeed, he had rarely even spoken of it to Smee—other than to tell the man that it was none of his business.

Jocelyn set aside the bag of coins and turned her attention to the map spread out before her on the writing desk. She brought her nose close to the paper and squinted, but it did no good. The map would share none of its secrets. A knock at her cabin door startled her. "Who is it?" the girl called, rather more gruffly than she intended.

"Roger Redbeard! Terror of the seven seas!"

Jocelyn flung open her door. Standing on the deck outside was a brown-skinned, curly-haired boy, who in just the last few weeks seemed to have passed her in height—though certainly not by much.

"Roger Redbeard, indeed? You look more like Roger

One-Whisker to me!" Her face broke into a grin, and she admitted the boy into her cabin.

"Really? I have a whisker?" Roger exclaimed, crossing to examine his face in the mirror.

"No. Not really." She giggled, feeling much happier than she had a few moments before. Roger always seemed to have that effect on her. She peeked over his shoulder, looking at his reflection. "I think that may be a bit of breakfast on your chin."

"No matter. One day it will be a full beard. You can't very well stop time." He turned to face her, pretending to stroke an impressively long beard. "I'll have more whiskers than Gerta!"

Jocelyn pictured the ruddy, stubbled face of the maid-servant she had been inflicted with at finishing school, before they came to the Neverland. "It is good to have ambitions," she said with a wink.

Roger gave a gentle tug to one of her curls. "Speaking of which"—he motioned to the map, unfolded on her desk—"still trying to make it spill its secrets?"

Jocelyn became very interested in a loose thread on her sleeve. "No," she mumbled. "Maybe."

The boy stepped toward the map, bending over to take a closer look. Jocelyn followed the movement of his eyes, knowing exactly what they would see. One large corner contained the edge of a landmass bordered by ocean.

The rest was a mess of squiggles and symbols, presumably coordinates and instructions, written in some kind of code. A code *without* a key. Roger, Jocelyn, and all the crew—with the obvious exception of Blind Bart—had each tried to crack it, to no avail.

Even though she knew it was of no use, the girl couldn't help but continue to stare at the map, hoping to find a clue she might have missed. There was something familiar about the bit of ragged coastline and the small river—or was it a creek?—penned on the page, but she couldn't place it. The Neverland changed so much and so often that even if she were to recognize the place, it certainly wouldn't look the same now. Without instructions, the adventure was over before it could properly begin.

"Any word from Smee's mapmaker acquaintance?" Roger asked.

"Not yet. I sent Meriwether again this morning to see if he has come back."

The pirate village boasted a single mapmaker. Mr. Smee had suggested that the former Captain Hook might have employed him in the creation of the treasure map. If that was the case, the mapmaker was almost certain to know how to break the code. Jocelyn and Roger, with the help of a generous sprinkling of fairy dust, had flown into the pirate village under cover of dark. Unfortunately, the pair had found his shop dark and shuttered, a sign on the door stating that the man was off on his annual kracken hunt and pillaging trip. There was no indication as to when he might return. Every few days Jocelyn sent Meriwether off to see if the mapmaker had come back, but as of yet, luck was against them.

Without any hope of breaking the code, Jocelyn's dreams of hunting for her father's treasure were becalmed as surely as a ship without wind. She had tried to take her mind off her frustrations by practicing her flying and exploring the island with Roger. They spent days in daring Neverland pursuits: hunting for bluecaps in an abandoned diamond mine, saying increasingly bad words in an attempt to summon Bloody Bones, and forcing an eyeless ghost to tell their futures. (Which was less exciting than it might sound. Their futures, as told, were rather mundane. To Roger: "Tomorrow you will spill juice in your lap." To Jocelyn: "You will fall asleep reading two nights this week.") Amusing as they were, those diversions were no longer helping. She wanted—no, *needed*—to go after the treasure.

A ringing bell interrupted her thoughts. Meriwether was back!

Jocelyn and Roger dashed out to the deck to greet the little blue fairy. He stuck out his tongue and gave Roger a pinch on the ear before settling onto Jocelyn's shoulder.

"Meri," she scolded, "leave Roger alone."

The fairy prince gnashed his teeth at the boy.

Knowing from experience that it would be unlikely

to do much good, Jocelyn didn't waste time on further reprimands. "What did you learn?" she asked. "Is the mapmaker in?"

Fairy language is very different from that of humans. To the untrained ear, it sounds like nothing more than the tinkling of bells. However, the more time Jocelyn spent with the little creature, the more easily she understood him. She thought it might have been because she had nearly been a fairy herself, if only for one night.

Meriwether nodded and jingled affirmatively, indicating that he had seen the mapmaker.

"Really? Are you sure?" Roger asked.

The fairy ignored the boy's questions and began polishing the buttons on his autumn-leaf jacket.

Jocelyn shrugged, making the tiny man bob on her shoulders. "I'm sorry, Roger. It is really quite silly of him to be jealous. Meriwether"—she turned her head to face him—"are you quite certain?"

Again his bells rang in the affirmative.

"Mr. Smee!" Jocelyn called out. "Tell the crew to prepare the ship! We enter the pirate village tonight!"

There are times when the wisest course of action is to throw caution to the wind and follow your own counsel. Those were the only times Jocelyn cared about. She sat in the galley polishing her sword in preparation for the night's adventure.

Mr. Smee joined her. "Beggin' your pardon, Captain, but if you'd like to steer us into port yourself, you may want to take the wheel. Blind Bart says he can hear cussing and spitting about three miles off. We're nearly there."

Blind Bart was Jocelyn's lookout, but since he chose to cover both eyes with patches (as a way to avoid seeing the ocean he so greatly feared), he relied on his unusually honed sense of hearing.

"Thank you, Smee," Jocelyn replied. She stood.

"Miss?" he said, before she left. "I know we've been over this a time or two, but I wouldn't feel right if I didn't say it once more."

Jocelyn sighed. She knew what was coming.

From the moment she'd found the map, Mr. Smee had been as nervous as a lobster in a pot, waiting for Captain Krueger to attack.

In case your memory is as short as your stubby, child-size legs, I'll remind you about Krueger: The man was a dark and ruthless pirate, cursed with an insatiable desire for gold. He would do anything and harm anyone to collect it. He had even gone so far as to pull his own teeth for their gold fillings, replacing them with razor-sharp points plucked from the mouths of baby sharks.

"I don't think the men should be set loose on the village on their own," Smee said. "They aren't ready. And with that black-hearted rogue Krueger thirsting for blood and treasure, and seeing that you have an abundance of one and a map to the other, I . . . that is, Johnny Corkscrew and me"—he gave a loving pat to the sword strapped to his side—"we think it wise for you to keep your distance as well. I could nip down to the mapmaker's real quick-like and even have time to pick up some supplies. You an' the crew could wait here for me to return."

If Jocelyn were being honest, she would admit she wasn't quite eager to meet Krueger again. She had already had one run-in with him, and it had been more than enough. The man had viciously attacked her ship under the mere suspicion the girl might have information about Hook's gold. Jocelyn had only escaped his sword when she fell overboard.

However, abject honesty aboard a pirate ship— particularly about one's feelings—is about as useful as woolen socks for a wooden leg. Jocelyn gave Mr. Smee's suggestion the tiniest bit of consideration before tossing it over the railing.

"Thank you for your concern . . ." she began. Mr. Smee gave her a hurt look. How it pained him when she was polite. She softened her speech with a "You filthy dog!" and continued: ". . . but the crew will be fine. *I* will be fine. We'll be careful. What could go wrong?"

What indeed?

The girl stood proud at the wheel of the *Hook's Revenge*, executing an almost-perfect docking just outside the pirate village. (She was certain no one would miss the last six feet or so of dock, as it had been, in her opinion, far too long to begin with.) Before disembarking, she took a moment to survey the village spread out before her in the early evening light.

Little had changed since she first set eyes on it. The beach was still crowded with row upon row of weathered docking. The gulls still screamed their shrill screams. The air was still ripe with the scents of brine, unwashed men, blood, and rotgut grog. The pirate village was still a veritable bouillabaisse of piratical atmosphere, full to the brim and running over. The only difference, really, was Jocelyn herself.

The last time she had visited, she had been a child on the brink of her first adventure and, like most children, so frightfully ignorant that she hadn't even known what to be afraid of. Since that time she had plunged into the depths of terror, been tested over and over, and in the end emerged victorious. I hardly blame her for squaring her shoulders and standing tall. I suppose she had earned a bit of posturing.

Get ready, pirate village, she thought. *Captain Jocelyn Hook has returned.*

Jocelyn strolled down the gangplank, her fairy on her shoulder, Roger at her side, and her crew close behind, looking every inch the captain she was. Even clad in the same ragged, threadbare dress she had been wearing so many weeks before on the night she first came to the Neverland, she exuded an air of authority and confidence. The island itself seemed to notice the young captain, hailing her triumphant return and framing her face with a sunset painted in pink and orange and blue.

Jocelyn stuck her tongue out at the pink.

The harbormaster waited at the bottom of the gangplank, ready to interrogate all new visitors to the pirate village. He held his lead pencil and ledger book at the ready, but the girl merely scowled at him. "I've no time for your questions just now; I've important business this evening."

He didn't argue, but stepped aside and tipped his hat. "Yes, miss, young Captain Hook. If I can be of assistance to you, please don't hesitate to call upon me."

She brushed past him without reply, eager to find the mapmaker and begin her next adventure. Roger gave a polite nod, but stuck close to Jocelyn in order to keep from being ensnarled in the man's bureaucratic red tape.

I've said it before and I'll say it again: That boy was a wee bit smarter than most. It's not saying much, but it's something.

At the end of the dock, Jocelyn turned to her crew. "All right, you dogs," she growled with a smile, "go show this town what you're made of. You've earned it. We'll meet back aboard the ship by first light."

"Tie the colors to the mast, boys! There'll be no

surrender tonight!" Dirty Bob called, and with many an *"Arrrrr!"* the men set off to celebrate their victories.

Mr. Smee stayed behind. He patted Jocelyn on the shoulder. "Do be careful, miss," he said, then set off toward his own tailor shop, turning just once to give a fretful look back.

Jocelyn grabbed Roger by the arm, pulling him in the opposite direction. "Come on," she said with a grin, "let's get this adventure under way."